Battling for Love:

A Celtic Law Novella

Second Edition

Battling for Love

A Celtic Law Novella

By: Brandi Baldesi

TATE PUBLISHING
AND ENTERPRISES, LLC

Published by Tate Publishing & Enterprises, LLC
127 E. Trade Center Terrace | Mustang, Oklahoma 73064 USA
1.888.361.9473 | www.tatepublishing.com

Tate Publishing is committed to excellence in the publishing industry. The company reflects the philosophy established by the founders, based on Psalm 68:11,
"The Lord gave the word and great was the company of those who published it."

Published in the United States of America

ISBN: 978-1-63063-989-1
1. Fiction / Romance / Fantasy
2. Fiction / Romance / New Adult
14.10.21

Nick thank you for the late night brainstorming and inspiration for which the base of this story would never have come to life.

The man who inspired my own love to get lost in and our beautiful daughter whom I hope one day will be a brave, independent, strong willed, and all around beautiful woman.

And lastly to my reader's thank you for taking a chance on me and picking my book off the shelf.

Prologue

I apologize now for my mindless rambling. There is much to tell and not much time to do so.

It seems like millennia ago…okay it was millennia ago but hey I am still in my prime here.

I may be a goddess, older than the world and its inhabitants. I may have watched the world transform and its people advance and develop but I, I am a goddess unaffected by time. I won't complain. I love that I will always be what people see as the source of youth and fun. I have had to adapt to changes over the many years though. Life now a day is nothing like the life I started in. Gone are the balls and festivals of old. The way of life and survival are altered and the language of the past is much forgotten and out dated.

Anyway, the easier times, when it was all about passion. War, Sex, and Love were the essence of passion then. Everyone was zealous about everything. This was when I thrived. I am Maeve, Celtic Goddess of War, Sexuality, and Intoxication, Goddess of Personal Power and

Queen of the Fey or Fairies as you call them now days. It's where I get my spritely youth from. I am a matriarch, mother, even a crone in some ways though much is forgotten about me in recent times. Who would care to think of a woman of old?

That's getting a little off track though. It may all seem like a party, something to be envious of to some but let me tell you now that you are wrong.

I caused wars through my incarnate Queen Maeve. The most famous was over a bull. Yes a bull, so stupid now but back in that time power was everything. I let the worst get a hold of me and I took it out on many people. Including the Queens daughter, who to an extent was my own daughter, I hurt her more than anyone and I have never forgiven myself. She was beautiful, young, fruitful and full of passion. She was so outspoken and carefree, at least when she wasn't in my presence or the Queens. She was the daughter after my own heart and my next incarnate. She loved a man so deeply and purely, and he returned that love in a way that was magical. I became resentful over the attention she was getting because I was use to every man fawning over me and I chased him away. You see I was a little selfish in those days. Every time she had a chance to be happy and almost left me I ruined her happiness. Eventually it ended in her death. I was so ashamed of myself and I still have yet to forgive myself for my intrusion that left me without a daughter that had so much potential.

I am the Goddess of Sexuality. I am beautiful, the essence of raw sexual need, and irresistible to almost every man. I was a Queen many times over, loved by many kings and their servants. It doesn't sound so tough but when you have a sexual desire that can only be sated after making love to 30 men a day, it becomes a problem. There was never any real love though for me it was only about sating my desire, for them it was bragging rights and power. Empty, meaningless sex, but don't get me wrong I enjoyed it. My men were always full of desire, and ready to please me no matter what. That's not the problem; my problem is I want one man who can do all those things for me, not 30. There is one man…well he is more than a man. He is Neit the

Celtic God of Battle. Ironic huh? The one man,

whom holds my heart, could be the answer to my dreams and fantasies is a God like me, all passion, power and strength. Only thing is he doesn't know the feelings I hold for him. I can't bring myself to tell him. You would think when one is my age they would have had many of those experiences. I haven't though. I guess you could say I have become picky in time. I don't want just sex. I want passion, love, friendship, companionship and something real. For someone like me, a Goddess, that is the hardest thing to obtain. Not even the Gods have the power to find something as pure as true love or a soul mate, it has to find us.

I envy you mortals. There are so many things you get to experience and feel that I do not. That is saying something when I am immortal and will exists for all time. You get to feel things I could only dream of. Even when I am with my ladies, incarnates, daughters if you will, I do not get to feel as they do. I only get to watch them feel and react. You get a last first kiss when you have found your soul mate and true love. That first kiss that will be the last because he will be the last one you ever kiss. You get to feel what it is like to die. Morbid, I know, but still I will never know how that is. You get to live life knowing that your experiences count. Every moment is beautiful and special. My life will never end, I get bored. I am bored! In all my time I have done so many things, I have watched the world change, seen man change, see time as it progresses but I will always have the same things, nothing new!

You mortals envy us because you want power and immortality but I am telling you now. I envy you! I would give anything to feel what you feel and experience life through your eyes. I want to feel true love, even if I will outlive that person and lose them. I want to have a near death experience that makes me cherish every day. Oh Goddess I sound so morose and miserable. I am really not. I won't bitch the whole time. I swear.

I just want to find a man worth it. To live and know life is good. I want something different. I am tired of being bored. If the Dagda (The Father of the Gods) could grant me one gift it would be one person to give me everything my heart desires and me be able to return it.

Unfortunately he refuses to grant me a selfish wish. If I want what my heart desires I need to help a mortal who needs me. He says it is his new law, the Celtic Law of the Gods.

….Well damn! Where am I going to find someone who needs me in a time when no one believes in me anymore….?

"Look into your heart my daughter. There is a part of you in a young girl on Earth. You have known her. You are reluctant to remember. You have spoken to her in your conscious. You know who I speak of. Her Irish blood calls to you. She has lost you, but she is calling to you. Go your answers lay there and before you worry, she is stronger than your last incarnate. She can prevail."

Well that was very subtle Dagda.

Chapter 1

"This is total shit!" Gilly thought aloud as she threw herself down on the bed not caring if she wrinkled the wedding dress she was trying on for the thousandth time. It was a beautiful gown. Really it was. Long and almost goddess like with hints of blue in the bodice. It brought out the blue in her eyes and complimented the golden sheen of her short blonde hair. She felt beautiful in it until she went down stairs to show Nicolai.

BATTLING FOR LOVE

Her "fiancée" had decided that he was going to control every little decision Gilly made and she could see her strength to fight for herself slipping away. This dress was the only part of the entire wedding and planning that she got to pick, it was her dream dress and Nicolai managed to crush that dream with one snide comment.

Gillyanna and Nicolai had come together as a business agreement. Nicolai needed a wife in order to prove to his parents that he could be taken seriously and she needed the connections he could give to help her writing career take off.

When she had first agreed to this arrangement it was because she had been fed up with being used and hurt by men. She thought this was the best way to protect her heart, but then she fell in love with the very man she had thought would protect

her from such an emotion. She didn't just fall in love, she was pretty sure he the one she would spend her whole life with. She had stuck with this agreement because she thought she could make him love her in return. Now she wasn't so sure.

BATTLING FOR LOVE

It was a constant rollercoaster with Nicolai. He always kept himself at a distance. He had a wall that he only put up when he was alone with her. She was trying to break it down. The few times he had let it down around her were some of the most amazing moments in her life. Those were the moments she had fallen in love with him and each time he slipped she fell more and over the past few months he had been slipping more and more.

His wall was breaking down and he knew it because when he would catch himself doing it he would put it back up and go back to being cold towards her. Around other people he wasn't as

guarded because he had to keep up appearances, he still kept a calm distantness but he was

more open to her. There were even moments when it felt like he was just as much in the relationship for the relationship as she was.

Where he took her out, made love to her and kissed her. She had taken advantages of those moments. She knew in her heart that if she could work through his wall she could reach his heart.

BATTLING FOR LOVE

There were times when she thought that she had, where she saw a tender emotion in his eyes. She just didn't know if it was love.

"Now, Now Gillyanna it can't honestly be that bad". Izett said as she tried very hard to hide the laughter in her voice.

She couldn't help but laugh when Gilly threw her little tantrums, they were quite entertaining. She sympathized with her best friend because she could see that womanly strength she always admired about her slipping out of her grasp.

She has always thought of Gilly as the strongest woman she had ever met, she had known her since they started high school and the friendship they quickly built has lasted almost 10 years, but she had never seen defeat in Gilly's eyes till now.

They grew up together in a sense. They

faced the hardest of teen years and heart breaks together. You couldn't break the bond they started at the age of 16. Hell at 26 they still held on to that sisterly connection. Izz and Gilly, two inseparable souls bound by an everlasting friendship, sisters in every way but blood.

Gillyanna turned to look at her best friend and scowled. She could see the humor in Izett's eyes but she could also see the troubled look there too. She didn't like either. She hadn't even realized Izett had followed her up to her room but she should have seen it coming.

Izett always managed to see her tantrums first hand. She was supposed to be the strong one, she hated being weak, but at least she knew she could be weak around Izett without being judged.

"Oh the hell it can't. Did you hear him down there? UGH! 'Gilly, do you really think that dress is appropriate?', 'Now darling, I know I said you could have a final say in the wedding arrangements but let's be real, my taste is exquisite compared to yours', God he makes me sick! Why did I even agree to marry him? Could you remind me?"

BATTLING FOR LOVE

The part that upset Gilly the most was that he had asked to see the dress at all. Wasn't it bad luck to see the bride in her dress before the wedding?

Plus his words hadn't reached his eyes; even as he insulted her with words he had assaulted her with a look of pure lust and desire. He liked the dress but she knew he wasn't going to admit it.

"Honestly, no. I have never liked mister 'I am so much better than you ever deserve'", Gilly snorted with laughter at how well Izett mimicked Nicolai's condescending tone," I think you said

It was because he was going to help you succeed and reach the top"

"Yeah, yeah. I remember," She did. Nicolai seemed to be the best man in town when they first met. He was well to do; he came from a good family, had money to offer security and had been so set on making her his wife.

He was the son of the town's most prominent lawyer so naturally she felt honored to stand at his side at first. Yet somehow over the last three years he had changed, and broke her spirits. She was tame, obedient and so damn boring now.

She was once so bubbly and free. She was always a hard worker but she lived by the motto "work hard, play hard". Somewhere down the line she forgot how to play.

"Well I am done. I am marching down there right now and shoving this "it cost me more than I should have spent on you" piece of shit ring down his throat." Gilly could feel the determination that shown through her fierce expression.

Izett's laughter followed her all the way down the hall and she couldn't help but smile when she heard her yell "knock the bastard on his ass Gilly". Just as she was about to burst into the living room and put him in his place, Izett came running down the stairs grinning wildly.

"I realized I couldn't miss the look on his face, and I know you're great with details but without a camera I need to witness this event so that I always have a memory to hold onto." Izett said as she caught up to Gilly in a fit of laughter.

"Izz, my dear sweet friend, I think my devious mind has worn off on you for too long." She couldn't even restrain the smile that took over her face when Izett stuck out her tongue like a child.

Gilly held onto that smile as she approached Nicolai. The fact that he looked suspicious only added to her sense of power. She hoped she looked innocent and genuine because that could only add to her fun honestly.

She was tired of holding back around him. It was time to let the shameless wench, as her father likes to call her, out. She looked at the man she had loved so deeply

The man who made her heart race and toes curl with just one stroke, even if those caresses were short and few and far between, she thought to herself. She wondered how his kisses would make her feel if he would give over to the passion they could share completely.

She looked into those blue eyes, the ones that held specs of green in them that reminded her so much of looking at the earth from space; she didn't feel like the world was at her feet anymore. She didn't feel anything at that moment but bitter resentment for the way he tried to make her something other than what she was.

"Did you come to apologize for running off like a child because you didn't get your

way?" The way he said that one sentence made her consider reaching out to claw him in the face. His patronizing, cool, detached tone made her skin crawl. How could she have put up with this for so long?

"Well I did come to apologize," the way she said it so calm and sweet made her want to laugh; she was a good little actress sometimes. She really wanted to lay him out. She hadn't kicked a guy's ass since she was 10 but she was losing control of the small bit of sanity that told her hitting him could end badly, "I came to say I am sorry that you are an ass. I am sorry that I ever conceded to marry you. I am sorry it took me this long to tell you what I think of you. You're the most arrogant, selfish, cold, hard man I have ever met and I want no part in being Mrs. Stick-up-my-ass."

If he hadn't been listening so carefully to her words he would have thought she had just given him the sweetest of compliments by the tone of her voice. It was so sweet and so soft he couldn't believe the insults that ran off her tongue. The worst part was how badly it broke his heart to hear her say those things. He loved the pert, loud, bubbly woman who stood before him staring him down. She was shorter than him by about a foot but in that moment she towered over him. Even now he thought her the most beautiful thing he had ever seen.

When he had set out to make her a part of his plan to get him into his father's firm, which he thought would be easy but they decided he needed to be a family man, he had expected Gilly to just go along and become the most perfect, dutiful of wives for the time being.

You know that line from that one song? A lady in the street but a freak in the bed? That's more of what he had in mind. Gilly on the other hand was the type of woman to say whatever she was thinking no matter the audience.

He didn't want to change her but he knew that if his plans were going to work he would have to, but just for now. That's why he kept himself at a distance.

He hadn't just chosen her out of nowhere, the first time he saw her in town he knew he wanted her. She was leaving the cafe with her friend Izett laughing a hearty, sultry laugh that made him want to be the one to put the smile on her face. He wanted that sound to roll over his skin and caress him for eternity.

She had coffee in one hand, waving her free hand about as she was talking and was making faces with Izett lost in their own little world. He walked closer to the women and introduced himself.

He even went as far as to kiss her hand like some kind of cad just to see her blush and when his eyes met hers he was lost. There was just something so special there. He thought it was just lust but after talking to her that first time he felt himself fall for her a bit.

Not that he would admit that to anyone aloud. He loved Gillyanna but he tried to ignore it, he had to put up a wall against her. He had to do what his parents asked. It was the only way to give Gilly the future she deserved.

It made him angry though when he thought about it, he had to push away the one person he wanted just to keep her and now here he was losing her.

"What did you just say to me?" He was angry at himself more than he was with her.

She saw the rage flash in his eyes and she started to take back what she said. It was killing her to say the things she was, after all she wanted this man. She loved him more than she ever thought possible. Then she thought about everything he had said to her to push her to this point and she didn't care. She wouldn't let him walk all over her. She was once so proud of her strength, of the feminine power she had. She wanted it back.

"You heard me. I have no desire to stay in this empty, meaningless relationship. Our deal is off. Here is your ring back. Now get out of my house."

"You have no idea what you're saying. This is a big mistake." Nicolai said frantically. He almost took it all back, almost apologized and told her the truth but he knew he could never take that back and he needed to keep control long enough to think of a new plan.

As he looked at her he could already sense that there was no way of keeping her at his side with the old reasons. She finally found the strength he had worked so hard to break, but his pride and rage wouldn't let her walk away so easily, neither would his love for her. He would win her back, he swore it to himself. He needed her, even if he couldn't admit it out loud.

"I thought that was how you would feel. However you have tried to make me into something I am not and I would never be happy with you." Even as Gilly said the words she felt the conviction in her words. She needed him to accept her as she was, to love her for all she was as a woman. "I need more than an arrangement. I need love, support and stability. You can't give me that."

"I need that too!" The words shook against his skull trying to break out of his head. He wanted to tell her she was wrong, that he was only trying to give her those things. He almost admitted his love for her.

He wanted to beg her to take it back and give him another chance but he had to choose his words carefully. It wasn't time yet; he needed to better himself first. He couldn't admit how he felt yet.

"Gilly, please think about this. This is a business agreement. You said you understood that. This can't be the end." He hoped she could see the silent plea in his eyes to get her to stay. The look that said his words were loaded, he couldn't say all he was thinking out loud.

"Actually it is. There is no "this" anymore. Now for the last time leave!" She saw a look in his eye she never had before. He looked sad but she was so angry with him she ignored it. She was even angrier with herself.

She couldn't believe all the things she gave up. All her dreams were wasted on him. Her love for him had turned bitter quickly. She didn't want it to and swore she would find away to get his love if it was the last she did, she just had to send him away first to find herself.

Then she realized something...her dreams could still come true. As she turned to Izett smiling, she reveled in the look of pure mischief her closest friend wore. Sometimes she loved how they thought so much alike.

Chapter 2

"Are we really doing this? I mean legit?" Izett looked at Gilly and laughed when she saw the look in her friend's eyes.

There was a mischief there that she couldn't help but fall prey to. She wasn't sure she believed in what they were doing but she did believe that her friend needed to do this for herself, to find her strength again. She needed Gilly to find that strength.

"Yes we are really doing this. So take off that damn robe, light the candles, and stop your bitching!" The way Izett acted all offended and grunted her response made Gilly giggle almost more than the words she actually spoke.

As Izett started to sing her own theme music and slowly strip out of her robe, making Gilly laugh harder, she started to prepare the circle to summon the Goddess Maeve.

Gilly tried to block out Izett's "I'm too sexy for my robe…Dah. Dah. Dah. dun dun dun" and

focus on the invocation of the Goddess she so
was so desperately seeking guidance from but
her mind kept wandering. She wanted so badly to
get past this weakness. She was so thankful for
Izett at the moment.

She needed that support. Finally ready to try
something new, to give in to the desperation,
Gilly shed her robe and joined Izett in
dancing naked under the stars.

They danced in circles twirling through the moon
light as it seemed to shine on them like a spot
light. Finally they collapsed on the ground

laughing their asses off trying to catch their breath.

"Oh goddess I cannot believe we just danced under the stars with everything our Mama's gave us out in the open." Gilly was trying to calm down and speak but her laughter kept coming.

"Have I told you lately how wonderful of a friend you are?"

"Well Gilly, now that you mention it, no you actually have failed to make that known, but I'll forgive you this once."

"Wow, I appreciate your understanding. Now that we have cleared that up are you ready to summon the Goddess?"

"Gillyanna, do you really think this will work? Do you really believe that this is the only option? I'm not trying to doubt you but seriously, this

isn't going to work, and your problems won't go away. You are the only one that can fix them."

"Izett, I understand where you are coming from, but I need to at least try. I can feel it. I am supposed to do this. If it doesn't work then I guess I have my answer."

"I thought that might be the case." Izz said and she got up and walked back to where she had set her belongings on the edge of the clearing. "So in the spirit of things, I have brought some libations in the name of the Goddess Maeve. Tada! A bottle of Mead for each of us."

Gilly leapt on her friend giving her the tightest hug she could manage. The fact that Izett was behind her on this completely made her so happy. She was tearing up by the time she let go.

"Now Gilly, I said a bottle *FOR EACH OF US*, no need to cry." Izett had that look on her face

that meant that this was to be one of those nights they never forget. She loved it. This is exactly what she needed. Her best friend, good wine, laughter and if the Gods allow it her guardian, the Goddess Maeve.

"Alright then Izz lets do this shit." Gilly laughed at herself, it felt so good to really laugh. "First we must create the circle. We have to summon from every direction calling each phase of the moon to us. Maeve is a goddess

under the full moon so we have to call that phase last."

"After you then friend."

Gillyanna took a deep breath, steadied herself, and took one last fleeting glance at her best friend for reassurance.

When Izett met her gaze with determination and handed Gilly the lighter she felt lighter and began to invoke the Goddess.

Gilly turned to the north of the circle and lit the first candle. "Power of the dark moon, deep and rich, you embrace us in your cloak of blackness, as the stars shine bright and sparkly. O wise grandmother, we invite you into our circle."

Izett then following Gilly's lead walking to the west and lighting that candle. "Power of the new moon, gentle and soft, you welcome us with open arms, as a new cycle begins. O sweet maiden, we invite you into our circle." Izz repeated the words Gillyanna taught her earlier in the evening

Gilly took her turn to the south. "Power of the waxing moon, energized and moving, you push me forward with sure hands, as I attain my deepest goals. O fierce warrior, we invite you into our circle."

Walking to the east Izett lit the candle there calling the waning moon to her. "Power of the waning moon, subtle and floating, you cradle us in your womb, as we heal our hurts and fears. O gentle queen, we invite you into our circle.

Meeting in the middle together they called the full moon in. "Power of the full moon, heavy and full, you empower my workings, as we align our energy with yours. O graceful mother, we invite you into our circle." As they lit their last candle wind picked up rustling their hair and the moon shown brighter on them.

BATTLING FOR LOVE

"Did you feel that Gilly?"

"Yea, what do you think that means?"

"I think it means you better invoke that goddess of yours." Izett couldn't believe what just happened. She wasn't quite sure what she felt, if she even felt it, but she knew Gilly believed and that had to be enough.

She gave Gilly a hug, kissed her on her cheek and sat down in the center of the circle. As she sat there she watched her friend in awe as Gilly started her ritual.

Gilly knew this was going to work. She wasn't sure how she knew it but she felt sure that the Goddess was already a part of her. She was connected to the Goddess, although she wasn't sure how she knew that either, now it was time to see what that bond meant.

She started to breathe deeply and slowly. She started to connect to the world around herself. Letting go of her body and focusing on the energy around her, she listened to the sounds that engulfed her, stretched her arms about her head centering herself, pulling herself back in. She opened her eyes and started to call the Goddess.

"Maeve: Red Goddess of Passion. The mare gnashes her teeth as her shoulder bleeds

warm and slick and pure. The stallion enters her pen as her secret chamber opens…."

Chapter 3

"You're being summoned Maeve."

Maeve turned from her window where she had been watching the young women dance and call to her to see Neit. The young God was standing behind her wearing that oh so handsome smile of his. He was her best friend.

He was the God of Battle and had been her companion in many wars fought in the past. He has stood by her side, her every decision and been her confidant when she needed a shoulder to cry on. She would have been lost without him.

Many of the Gods had thought them to be lovers for as long as she could remember. No one believed that she had not tried to have her way with him. Maeve understood why too. Neit was gorgeous. His blonde hair hung just past his shoulders in flowing waves. His eyes were a hazel with specs of yellow in them that turned gold when he was in battle. His lips full and kept in a tight scowl he but even that was handsome.

He was large and bold, his body the essence of taut muscle, from his broad shoulders to his legs. His skin was the only dark part of him, but even that golden darkness was alluring. He was beautiful.

She always appreciated the way he looked. She yearned for him too. Sometimes the way he looked at her made her blood run hot and made her mind wander to things that almost made her blush…almost. She often caught herself wondering if he was capable of feeling the things she felt for him in return but was quick to banish those thoughts for she knew he would only see her as a companion on the battle field and a friend. She wasn't exactly sure what she wanted from him but she did know she would need him as more than a lover.

She loved him that much she was sure about. She just couldn't tell him out of fear that he would reject her.

"I know. I was but watching. It is nice to see someone remembering me and the righteous way of summoning me." She looked back out her window and felt Neit step up behind her.

She glanced over her shoulder and noted how close he was. She felt her breath catch in her throat; he smelt as good as he looked. His was the smell of a true man. Musky, powerful, manly and strong in the best possibly sense.

"She is a part of me. She calls to me I can feel her pull. We are connected."

Neit took advantage of her distracted state. As he came up behind her he was entrapped by the smell of her. She smelt of honey. The mead so named after her was an essence of that sweet nectar. There was something else there too.

Something womanly and seductive but he wasn't sure he could place the scent off hand.

He knew it was dangerous to be so close to her.

He wanted her; she didn't even have to try. He knew that everyone around them already thought them lovers but he wanted it to be true.

No, he wanted more than that. For more years then he could care to remember he had been in love with Maeve and had to sit back hoping that one day she would take notice.

So many times the words that would reveal all he felt had been on the tip of his tongue but pride kept them from being spoken. He was so afraid that she wouldn't return what he felt. Stepping closer to her he finally realized what the sweet, intoxicating smell that rolled off her was.

"Roses!" She smelt of honey and roses! By Gods what a mix! Just the smell of her made him tight with need. He had kept himself at a distance for so long but he could feel that distance shrinking. This could not be good.

Maeve was startled by his outcry. Turning to face him she gasped. His eyes were almost completely gold which was confusing in itself since the only time she could recall that happening was when he was in the troughs of battle. She was confused by this more than by his exclamation.

"Roses?" She didn't understand what he had meant but her curiosity was sparked.

"Yes, um roses. Take her roses when you finally reveal yourself. The yellow ones that you love so much…use them to make your grand entrance."

Oh nice cover. She probably saw right through that one. I am an idiot!

"What a divine idea Neit! I will!" Maeve threw herself in his arms and hugged him. Has she not he would have seen the smile that she wore and she would have to explain the reason. How she

would do that without laughing out right would
be hard.

He was turning pink! A blush was

making its way up from his toes she could swear
on it. Was he embarrassed? She laughed a little
as she buried her face in his neck.

When he grew tense she started to pull away
feeling as if she crossed some invisible boundary
between them. As she started to remove herself
from his arms his hold on her tightened, she

almost groaned aloud as she was pulled taut against his broad chest but caught herself.

Slowly he started to release his hold and she had to stop herself one more time from groaning out loud but this time from disappointment. It felt so good to be in his arms. She wasn't ready to let go.

"Yes, well, off you go then and good luck my dear friend" Neit was reluctant to let go of her.

It felt right to have her in his arms. Her body was pressed so tight against his, he was afraid she would feel the proof of desire he was gallantly sporting. He could still feel her on him. He didn't want to let go but if he didn't he knew he would give into that desire.

He wanted to kiss her, he wanted to push her down and make love to her. To show her in all ways the love he had kept bottled up for so long. He knew her past, sometimes he resented it but he knew her old ways had died. She wanted one man to love. He just wished he could be that man.

Maeve almost hated the way he called her friend, but she had come to expect it. While the word played over in her head repeating itself like a nightmare she realized she needed to leave. Not only because she could feel the pull from Gilly but she needed space from Neit before she threw herself at him.

She had never allowed herself to be that close to him. In fact that was the first hug she had shared with him in the entirety she had known him…that meant millennia. She couldn't shake the feelings it had risen in her. Just that one hug had made her desire spike.

She needed to be more careful because if she wasn't she was going to be in a world of hurt from wanting him.

"Okay…off I go then. I can feel the pull of my daughter even now. I will find you as soon as I return…friend."

"I'll be keeping an eye out for you" The way she had said the word friend held a hint of bitterness he didn't understand.

He felt his hopes raise but quickly beat them down. He knew it was stupid to let hope get in the way. He had meant what he said too.

He would be keeping an eye out for her but he was also going to keep an eye on her. He was always protective but even though he didn't know what had just passed between them he felt the need to watch her in hopes of learning more. She would open up to her new friends, he was certain of it.

He would be eavesdropping. He just hoped it wouldn't be in vain and that she wouldn't be mad when she found out.

Chapter 4

"Maeve: Red Goddess of Blood. Your warriors stain the ground as their life force flows. The earth welcomes their wholesome gift as she embraces your womb milk and honors your strength..."

Gilly was putting everything she had into this invocation. She desperately needed this to work. She knew she was connected to the goddess. She could feel it. She just needed it to work. She felt so weak and the goddess was her last resort. She could see Izett sitting off to the side and knew that her best friend was giving her all her faith.

She was feeding off that energy. Her voice was growing louder and stronger. The exoneration in her speech gave her courage. She not only felt what she was saying, she also believed it. She threw her hands up and looked to the moon.

"Maeve: Red Goddess of Power, the spirit burns bright as painful decisions come to light…"

Izett was watching Gilly in awe. She couldn't believe what she was seeing; yellow roses were popping up all around the circle Gilly was dancing in. Gilly's skin was glowing a honey color that made her look like a goddess herself.

"Gilly...I think it is working!"

"Bringing tears and sorrow. The mantle rests heavy on your shoulders..." "Gilly!"

"As you straighten your crown and smile..."

"Gillyanna McFly! Stop and look around you! It's working!"

Gilly abruptly stopped when she heard Izett scream her full name. She turned around to look at her friend and saw Izett looking dumbstruck and in awe. She didn't understand.

She had to finish the last part of the invocation. She turned back to start again and something caught her eye. She looked down at herself to see a honey glow. Then she spotted something yellow on the ground around her. She looked all around and saw yellow roses everywhere in the circle. She looked back at Izett.

"Izett! Roses! I'm fucking glowing!"

"Yea I see that Gilly. I was trying to bloody tell you that! It's working. Finish the invocation!"

"Right, right. Where was I?"

"Crown and smile! Crown and smile!"

Gilly was so excited. It was working. Holy shit! It was working! She had to pull it together though. She kept losing her train of thought. Izett said crown and smile…what came next?

"Izett I can't remember what comes next!"

"Legit? You're the only one that knows! Think Gilly! Think!"

 "I am trying here!" Gillyanna couldn't wrap her head around the words to was dumbstruck.

Maeve: Red Goddess of sex, of flow, of Sovereignty.

Gilly heard a husky, sultry, womanly voice in her head and looked around.

She couldn't figure out where it was coming from.

"Izett, did you say something?"

"What are you talking about? No. I couldn't even find the words to tell you that your ass was all aglow!"

Gilly was confused. She knew she had heard a woman's voice. It was a familiar voice. She was quickly reminded of the times she had heard the voice before. Times when things had been rough for her, when she thought she was all alone.

Then she realized that this was the voice she had always called her voice of reason. Her own little Jiminy Cricket!

Gillyanna McFly. You know me. You know we are connected. Finish the last part of your invocation so I can show myself to you. You know the words.

"Holy Shit! You're in my head. You're in my head. Izett! The goddess is in my head!"

Ha-ha Yes Gillyanna I am. I have always been. You've heard me before long ago. Finish calling me to you my daughter.

Gilly heard that laughter and it was music to her ears. It was the same laughter she had heard echo at her most pert moments in life. The moments when she reprimanded herself for things she had said. It was the laughter that let her known she was allowed to think as she wanted and speak her mind. She had missed that laughter.

"I remember the words!"

"Well good for you, get on with it already!"

Ignoring Izett's sarcastic remark Gilly finished her invocation.

"Maeve: Red Goddess of sex, of flow, of sovereignty, Red Goddess of childbirth, of dreamtime, of calamity. Red Goddess of life, and death, and uncertainty. Your power speaks to me. I bring it into myself with every

breath, with every sigh, with every laugh with every cry!" Gilly said the last verse aloud and as powerful as she could. She threw her arms above her head shouting in joy.

Izett was startled when all of a sudden a beautiful woman appeared next to Gilly. She was the most beautiful woman she had ever seen. Before her stood a woman with blood red hair down to her waist, wild and uncontrollable. She was a shorter woman but had all the womanly curves a man could ever lust for and any other woman would be envious of.

She had long shapely legs, rounded hips, a slim waist, fulsome rounded breast that were the perfect proportion to her body and soft gentle shoulders leading to a delicate neck. What caught Izett's attention most of all was her eyes.

They were the palest blue eyes she had ever seen. Almost as clear as a flowing stream.

Her smile was soft and inviting. Full, red lips and soft rosy cheeks brought a tempting color to her face. There was no denying that this was the woman that represented sex. She was slightly envious of the woman before her. It wasn't until she was done studying the Goddess that she noticed the Goddess looking at her intently.

Izett, you have done me proud by standing by my daughter's side all these years. She has needed you more than you know. I will forever be grateful. You are a woman of great beauty and I wish you could see that in yourself. Although you are not my incarnate as your friend is you are of my own blood and power I have use

for you yet. You are connected to me in a
powerful way. You shall see.

Izett heard the Goddess in her head and nodded her response. "Thank you Maeve," was all she could think. She wasn't sure she understood what the Goddess had meant but her words sounded sure and honest. All she could do was sit back and wait for the Goddess to show her what she meant. She then looked at her best friend and truly saw her for the first time since the Goddess had shown herself. Gilly might have been a more beautiful sight then Maeve; however she would not tell the Goddess that she thought slyly.

Gilly felt the Goddess before she even opened her eyes to look. She knew it had worked. She finally understood why she had held such a powerful belief in this one Goddess even though she couldn't give a sound argument as to why.

Finally opening her eyes she turned to the glorious woman standing next to her. She had seen this beautiful lady before in her dreams. She now fully comprehended what that meant but she couldn't voice it. She started to cry.

"Gillyanna say it. I know what you are thinking and I need you to put your voice to it." Maeve looked at the young woman that was to be her next incarnate with tears rolling down her cheeks. She had known since the day Gilly had entered the world. She also knew she had to wait for Gillyanna to come to her. It was the hardest part. She almost broke the rules a few times, wanting to come to Gilly's aid when things became too hard for her. She had to settle with little bits of whispered inspiration and confidence.

She had almost given up hope when Gillyanna had lost her strength thanks to Nicolai. She couldn't even describe the joy she felt when Gilly had turned him away.

Now she needed Gillyanna to take up her part, to accept her destiny.

"You've been with me my whole life. I have felt your presence many times, heard your voice, and seen your face. You are no stranger to me. That can only mean one thing; I am a part of you. That makes me your incarnate, does it not?"

Even as Gilly asked that question with uncertainty, she felt the true answer. She was the incarnate of the Goddess Maeve. That is why she had such strength. It's why she was drawn to

Maeve. It is also explained her obsession with Mead, she thought laughing to herself. What it made her realize next is what hurt the most.

She had always believed in the Goddess and Nicolai had made her feel that her belief was wrong, he never supported it and that is why she had slowly lost her faith in her Goddess and her strength.

"Yes, my daughter, you are. You are the missing piece of me. You have always been a part of me, and me of you. You have all my strength and more. That is why I have heeded your call. I have waited many years for you to come to me Gillyanna. I have watched you grow into the strong woman you are. It pains me to know you have lost some of the feisty power you had. My only regret is that I couldn't come to you sooner.

To teach you all I know and keep you from the pain you had felt."

Gilly felt the tears running down her cheeks. So many things in life were starting to make sense but now she felt as if all this pressure was just added to her. How was she supposed to live up to the Goddess?

She didn't think she could. She had strength and confidence but not for this. Not to have a woman who stood above all others say she was a part of that. She felt like a contradiction of things. She was happy and sad, relieved and overwhelmed, scared yet excited.

Nothing made sense but yet it all made perfect sense. All the dreams, visions, voices and unexplained things from her childhood were all falling into place and she finally understood.

"I don't think I can do it Maeve. I think you have the wrong girl." Even as Gilly saw the look of fury cross the Goddesses face she knew she had spoken wrongly. She had just questioned the one woman who would know all truths in her life. Not to mention a Goddess known for her temper.

"Gillyanna! What the hell is wrong with you?"
Izett finally broke out of her trance.

She had caught what Gilly had said and it made
her furious, she couldn't even imagine how
furious Maeve was but from the look on her
face it wasn't looking good for Gilly.

"The Goddess Maeve herself shows up because
YOU call her and you have the nerve to question
her? That's blasphemous! I'm really hoping it
was shock that made you say such things

because frankly this isn't the Gilly I know and I'd like her back. Right this damn minute!" Izett was breathing heavily and her rage was at its heights. She had never been so angry before. Hell she had never yelled at Gilly like that before.

Gilly and Maeve were both gaping at Izett. The fiery little red head that had always had a temper had never once raised her voice like that before and they both knew it. They were both stunned. Gilly could not believe what just came out of her dear sweet Izz.

Never had Izett ever spoken like that to anyone. She was proud that Izett had finally stood up and spoke her mind completely but at the same time she was stunned and upset that she had been the one to bring that out.

Maeve stared at Izett in disbelief. She knew that the young woman had it in her but she hadn't expected her to let it out tonight. Everything was falling into place and she couldn't wait to reveal her plans for the girl but knew she had to wait till Izett revealed more; she knew she had been right in setting these two young ladies paths in the same direction.

She was vainly proud of herself for cheating fate and bringing such wonderfully strong, beautiful, passionate, women together to full fill a destiny that would be hard to compete with. She had waited a very long time to find out if Izzet had what it would take for the journey she had planned for her.

"Now, it seems I was wrong about you Izett. You are one of my own, a daughter after my own

BATTLING FOR LOVE

heart." Her laughter was soon filling the air all around them.

Izett just looked at her, smiled and started to dance around again laughing and shouting.

It didn't take long before Maeve threw off her gown and she and Gillyanna joined in; their rich, sweet, seductive laughter reaching the heavens.

103

Chapter 5

Neit looked out the window and down at the women in the grove. He was shocked when the little red haired one raised her voice and yelled at her friend Gillyanna, leaving both girls pale and gaping slightly. When Maeve just smiled at the girl and called her daughter he relaxed.

He knew Maeve would find all she needed in those two young women down there. She would have friends to keep her company during her time on earth. He just hoped that she would need him still; better yet want him when this was all over.

Suddenly all of his attention was drawn to Maeve, her wonderful laughter reaching his ears like the beautiful song of an angel. He had always loved the sound. It shook him to the bones, warming him from the inside out. His body grew taut just from hearing it. His need for her apparently was out of his control.

"Damn it!" He frowned and ran his fingers through his thick blonde hair as he turned from the window. The tension in his body even reaching his rough, battle worn hands, he needed to distance himself from her. He needed to stop this wanting. "And I will. No matter what it takes, I have to stop wanting her. It's been too many years of sitting by waiting. If I have to I will leave."

Turning back to the window and the women below his breath caught in his chest. Maeve had just shed her robe and was dancing around with the other women. He had never seen Maeve completely naked before.

He had always tried to respect her by turning away although it killed him to not look over his shoulder when she dressed. As he stared at her he didn't think he had seen anything as beautiful as what he was seeing now.

"By Gods she's the most glorious thing I have ever laid eyes on. If only she knew what she was doing to me!" If it was even possible he felt his body grow tighter. He was all firm, molten heat, hard but silken.

He focused his gaze on Maeve; he studied all he could see starting from the ground up. Maeve was poise and beauty. She had small dainty feet that were soft and petite. Her legs were slender and long but muscular and strong, the build of a warrior. Forcing himself to overlook the glory that lay at the junction between her legs he continued to look up.

Her waist was all curves and softness but her stomach was flat and tight, probably from all of the training and fighting she had done her whole life.

Her breasts were not very large but they looked like they would fit into his hands nicely. They were round and nicely shaped with honey colored tips that he could only imagine tasted just as they looked. Licking his lips he glanced upward to her beautiful face. She wore a smile that he could only wished was directed at him.

Her deep red hair fell all around her in a shear glow illuminating like a fire. Her well-shaped back side resembled a heart and wiggled as she moved.

Finally he let his eyes rest on the little patch of heaven between her legs. His breath quickened when he finally saw what lie there. It was a stunning patch of curls the same fiery temptation as the hair on her head. He couldn't wait to bury himself in them, to show her in all ways that he loved her, to touch every inch of her and make her his.

He couldn't stop himself from picturing all the ways he would do that. They were fantasies he had been suffering from for thousands of years, they haunted his dreams. The ways he would slowly take her, show her what it was like to be loved by a God like him.

He'd make sure no other man could even be compared. He would let her know that he was the only man she would ever need or have again. She would welcome him with open arms into her tight, wet, heat and let him love her. He let out a long low growl at the thought as he found his release and fell to his knees.

It was then that he realized he had been pleasuring himself. He had been so captivated by the sight of her and his needs and his emotion he hadn't noticed. He had been picturing all the ways he would love her and got lost in that passion.

"Well shit." He got up and walked away from the window and cleaned himself up. He knew now that his need for her, his love and all he wanted from her would keep him by her side. Keep him fighting for her love. He was the God of Battle and this was a battle he intended to win, he would win.

His gaze swept across the clearing to the edge of the woods where he saw movement. He had some of the sharpest eyes of any of the Gods, that is one reason he did so well in battle. He focused his attention on the movements and noticed it was a man. At first his rage consumed him, bubbling to the point of bursting. His first thought was that this man was watching his woman...his woman...he had already become possessive. Then he watched the man closer and noticed that it was Nicolai.

This man was Gilly's ex. His rage reduced to a simmer. He was still angry about this man watching the women but he had been doing the same himself. It also helped that Nicolai's gaze was fixed on Gillyanna, unwaveringly so.

Neit realized that then that the man had a look of want in his eyes. He was confused by it but he did understand that Nicolai loved Gilly. The look in his eyes said that much.

As he watched Nicolai struggle to leave, he decided he might have a way of getting closer to

Maeve. He could also help this man gain Gilly back, because from what he had seen and heard, she still loved Nicolai. He knew he shouldn't mettle but he would. He had just found a loop hole and was going to take advantage of it.

He was going to take this young man under his arms and protection. If Maeve was allowed a human incarnate so was he. He had been watching Nicolai for years since he was always around Gilly while Maeve watched her daughter.

Nicolai had a fighting spirit about him and many of the same qualities that Neit himself possessed. He had often thought that if Nicolai could figure out what he wanted and think for himself he would be the perfect son to have on earth.

It also helped that Neit had been waiting for Nicolai to come around. Nicolai was to Neit what Gilly was to Maeve. Neit had been waiting many years for the boy to finally become the man he needed to be.

"I have found my son and now he will follow my lead on earth, now all I have to do it get through to the stubborn ass and help him open his eyes to what he needs not just what he wants. Maeve's incarnate is right for him; he just needs to see it completely. I just hope Maeve isn't angry about my being so close on this…maybe she doesn't have to know…" he knew that it would be impossible to keep it hidden from her but he was going to try.

He had been keeping the connection he had with Nicolai and the facts from the past that the

Dagda had told him secret for 28 years now, surely this one last thing wouldn't be so hard to keep to his self. With his mind made up and his determination fueling him Neit walked away from the window to prepare for his stay on earth.

Chapter 6

The women collapsed in a circle while still being held by a fit of giggles, the moon shown down bright and clear all around them lighting up the clearing just to the edge of the woods. If it had reached just a little farther they might have been able to see Nicolai standing there in the shadows where he had been watching the three women, although his focus never left Gilly.

She was incredibly beautiful. He had always thought so but tonight she glowed. No really she was glowing! Her skin was a honey golden color, she looked beautiful but he had always preferred her milky fair skin.

He had come to Gillyanna's to convince her to stay with him. As he approached the house and rang the bell he wondered if they would open the door for him. When no one answered he started to walk around back checking in all the windows as he went. As he reached the backdoor he had heard laughter coming from the woods behind the house.

He suddenly remembered a clearing back that way where he and Gilly had once had a picnic, it was the last place he had made love to Gilly. The only place he had allowed his emotions to show through. Pushing back that memory he followed the path to the clearing.

As he got closer to the clearing the laughter became louder and he realized that Gillyanna wasn't alone. He almost turned around but his curiosity took hold. He came to the clearing stopping just at the edge of the shadows and saw three women running around naked. At first he thought he was dreaming. Then he looked closer and saw that two of the women were Gilly and Izett.

His gaze quickly landing on Gilly and not wavering, muttering a string of curses he looked at her beauty. It wasn't hard to see that Gilly had found that strength again and that was something he found so sexy.

He thought back over the years and could only recall a few times when he was happy with Miss Gillyanna McFly. The worst part was it was his fault entirely not hers. There were times when he let his guard down around her, when he was completely natural around her and he was able to see her for the beautiful person she was.

At those times he could see himself being happy with her. He would fall for her a little bit each time those moments came around and each time he caught himself he would put the wall back up. The worst part was the hurt in her eyes.

She really had loved him. Despite all of the jerk things he did and no matter how much of an ass he was at times she loved him because of his moments of vulnerability. She had clung to those moments and held on tight. When he would flip the switch and go back on guard he could see her heart break in those beautiful grey eyes.

He loved her eyes. You could see into her soul through them. Every emotion, every thought was shown through them. She was an open book and he had tried to rewrite her.

BATTLING FOR LOVE

He felt guilty about all of it. He was at a constant battle with himself. He wanted to fix things but the timing wasn't right. He knew in his heart she was his mate, the one he was meant to be with.

He didn't know why it took him so long to finally see this all straight. At first he thought she would just go along with the plans and be the most dutiful of wives. She had played the part well in the beginning but she had to fight it and push him to this point for him to see what he really wanted. He wanted the impertinent, bubbly, silly, wild, carefree woman he had found her to be. She was beautiful, smart, kind and all around happy...until he tried to break her. He wanted to walk right into the clearing and let her know what he really wanted but he would buy his time, and as he did he would keep his eyes out for the three women. Something was off.

There was something not quite right about the new angel keeping company with Izett and Gilly and he was going to find out what it was. He turned to walk away and as he did he heard the

the women starting to talk. Pausing in his steps he listened carefully.

"Maeve, I am so thankful you answered my call.

I have been so lost without you. I never should have let Nicolai turn me away from you. I was blinded by the love I wanted and what I had hoped would be a good future with him. I didn't see how wrong I was till it was too late."

Nicolai recognized Gillyanna's velvety voice instantly. The things she had said hurt him because he never wanted to hurt her and to hear her once again voice the pain he caused her made him livid. But what caught his attention the most was the name she had called the woman she spoke to.

Maeve…he hadn't heard that name in a long time. It was the name of a Goddess Gilly had talked about obsessively at the start of their relationship. None of this was making any sense.

"Gillyanna, my daughter, you never turned away from me completely. If you had, I wouldn't be here now. Yes you let a weak man weaken you but you found the strength again. That is all I care about." The woman named Maeve had a voice thick and rich like honey. There was a sweetness, yet powerful strength in her words.

Nicolai realized that he would have a harder time getting close to Gillyanna now, because he was certain she was under the protection of the Goddess. The Goddess he tried to turn

her from, his outlook wasn't looking to good now. Confidence fully shaken now he turned and walked away.

He went up to the house and wrote a note for his love. He liked the sound of that…his love. He finished the note sealing it and sticking it by the back door and continued the walk back to his car. He got in and sat their looking at Gilly's quaint country home; it was the place he wanted to be in her arms, loving her and sharing every moment with her.

He could see them having a family there and growing old there together. He needed to fix things and soon, he didn't think he could stay away for long.

"I will win her back no matter the challenge. I need her. She is my other half and I can't walk away. Damn the consequences." And with that he peeled out of the driveway to make his changes.

Chapter 7

The women made their way back to the house. As they started walking they were full of chatter and laughter over everything that had happened but slowly they settled into companionable silence.

They walked arm in arm staring ahead into the darkness that the surrounding woods created. As the lights from the house came into view they heard a car start and peel out. Gillyanna took off

running to try to catch whoever it was. Maeve
and Izett running up on her heel.

She reached the drive just in time to see

Nicolai's SUV speeding away. "What the hell
was he doing here" was all she could think. Then
her fears took hold. What if he saw them? Was
he spying on her?

With that last thought she turned and bolted to
the house. She knew as soon as she reached the
door her fears had been wrong. She started to

think he had come to reconcile but she beat down that thought too. She needed to keep her head clear. Maeve and Izett had just reached the driveway as she darted past them making them stumble a bit in their pursuit.

She reached the back door twisted the handle to find it still locked; she breathed a sigh of relief and looked down. There she saw a note and looked at her friends as they finally reached the door, both panting and gasping for air. Gilly hid the note in her robe and turned to them.

"What the hell Gilly?" Izett spoke first looking at Gilly as if she were insane.

"Sorry, I was trying to catch the car." Gilly was about to tell them that the car had been Nicolai's but something made her bite her tongue. She still had to find a way to get him to open his heart to her. She would be with him again; she just couldn't tell her friends that.

After everything, she still loved the man he was capable of being. She just hoped he could be that man again.

"You thought you could catch a car?" Izett first looked at Gilly in disbelief then at Maeve with a questioning look. As she met Maeve knowing look she realized that Maeve knew something she didn't. She started to ask but Maeve subtly shook her head no. Izett, don't question her on this.

There is a battle going on in Gilly's heart and only she can fight it. She is going to need you there to support her but wait until she opens up to you on this one.

Izett gave a nod and looked back at Gilly. "Well, did you see who it was?"

Gillyanna looked at both of the women before her and felt guilty about the lie she was about to tell but she knew in her heart that Izett wasn't ready to hear what she was planning. She needed Izett to fully accept what she had to do, something she knew Izz couldn't...no wouldn't be ready to do.

"No, I didn't. Guess I was too damn slow." Gilly met Maeve's gaze and knew that her Goddess could see the truth behind her words. *I'm sorry Maeve, she just isn't ready. I know you can see what I want, what I am planning, but Izett can't know yet. I'm begging you please don't tell her. I know you may not agree with this either but I need to do this for me.*

She knew Maeve understood just by the look in the woman's eye but was relieved when she heard the Goddess whisper in her head, *Do not worry my sweet child, I stand by your choices. I have a plan of my own.* Gilly looked closely into the eyes of her Goddess and saw the wheels turning there and smiled. Her attention was quickly returned to Izett though because Izett started to speak.

"Well is the house still locked? Is everything Okay? Ideas on who it could have been?"

"Izz! This isn't 50 questions...calm down. The house is fine, no one broke in. Everything is okay. And no I don't know have any idea who it was." Gilly thought for a second that Izett was going to press for more answers but she saw Maeve silence her friend.

She had a feeling Maeve was playing mediator in this situation and when Maeve just winked at her she knew she was right.

She opened the back door and walked into her kitchen. She was considering whipping something up because cooking always helped her clear her mind almost as well as writing could.

Both of her friends followed her and took seats at the island in the kitchen. There was some more small talk and laughter and Gilly made up some pasta and salads for them all. The silence that overcame them all as they ate allowed her mind to roam and she didn't welcome it. She kept thinking about the note in her pocket…the one from Nicolai. Once again Izett was the one to break the silence.

"Maeve, are you staying here or going back?" Izett looked at both women for an answer.

"Well Izett, I could easily just come and go as needed. My realm over looks this area but I had rather hoped I'd be welcome to stay here with

Gilly." Maeve looked at her Daughter giving her the chance to decide and think.

"Maeve, I am going to need you here all the time. I can't do this alone. It would be comforting to know that you're right down the hall. I want you here with me so yes please stay."

Maeve looked at Gilly and glowed. For the first time in her entire existence she had girlfriends.

Chapter 8

Gilly wished her friends a good night and ran up the stairs to her room, clutching the note from Nicolai to her chest. She had been restless ever since she picked it up. She knew that her friends could sense it so she tried very hard to contain it but she couldn't take her mind of it.

She had finally broken away from them for the night and was ready to find her solitude and lose herself in Nicolai's words. Part of her was afraid that the note contained words of resentment and animosity, bring to life her worst fear…the one where Nicolai wouldn't be able to return her affection. The other part of her was giddy, like some love struck teenaged virgin who just received a note from her crush saying "I like you will you go out with me…circle yes or no". She laughed at her own thoughts of irrationality.

She reached her door and turned the knob gently. Her fears had taken hold of her in those last few strides. She was in a relentless conflict with her heart and head. She wandered to her bed and turned to plop down on the edge, pulling her legs up tight to her in an effort to ease her anxieties. She stared at the note in her hands and set it to the side of her. She kept trying to decide what to do. Open it, don't open it. Read it, throw it away. What to do? She was so confused.

Gilly, your thoughts are all over the place. They are screaming at me from down the hall. You're going in circles. If you don't read it now it will eat at you and you will always wonder. You are strong, remember that. This note doesn't mean an end or beginning. You decide that. You don't have to give up. I love you my daughter, breathe and read the damn thing.

Gilly sent a quiet "Thank you" to Maeve. She took a few deep breaths, calming herself, centering herself. She even went as far as calling the phases of the moon to her for extra strength.

With Maeve's support and the moons power behind her she reached for the note and opened it so that it was facing away from her.

She opened it fast and quick…like the removal of a Band-Aid. Taking one last breath, holding it deep in her lungs, she flipped the note so that the words faced her.

Sweetling,

I am so sorry. I hope you can find it in your heart to forgive me. I will make this all up to you. I know I don't deserve this but please wait for me to figure something's out. I will be back for you, I love you Gillyanna.

Love your, Boy-o

Gilly stared at the note in her hands. She felt the tears running down her cheeks but she didn't try to stop them, she let them fall. She wasn't ashamed. He loved her. He admitted it. She knew he loved her, she had seen it on a few occasions, but to have him put it so plainly made her heart clench. She sent Maeve her thoughts, sending her a mental picture of the note. She liked being able to communicate with her Goddess this way.

She got a simple reply this time, *Patience*. She was confused at first then realized Maeve meant patience for Nicolai, for the things he had to do and patience for herself in waiting. She kept wondering what all he had to do, and how long it would take him. She had no doubts about how long she would wait. Nicolai was the one; she would wait for a lifetime if she had too.

She was sucked out of her thoughts when her phone started playing Faith Hill's "Take Another Little Piece of My Heart". It was Nicolai's ringtone, at first she just listened and realized just how ironic it was. After it stopped playing she reached for the phone to check her texts.

She opened his message and it read;

Did you get my note?

She grinned to herself while trying to think of what to say. She ran through a few dialogs in her head but settled for something she thought would give him the answer to the question he was really asking…**I love you Boy-o**

She wasn't the least bit surprised when she received an answer back right away.

I love you too Sweetling. I have so much to explain to you. I should have done it sooner, but not in a text. I miss you, I will fix this and I promise you a future you deserve.

She was in tears again but this time because her heart was finally feeling well…right. She just had to have the strength to wait for him. She let him know that in her response.

Waiting my love.

He sent one last reply; she hadn't expected a reply to that one.

You won't need to wait long baby girl because I can't stand the idea of not being there. I feel horrible about how I treated you. I will spend the rest of our lives making it up to you.

She sent her final reply before she got up to turn off the light for bed.

You're off to a great start. Goodnight. Take all the time you need. I refuse to give up on you. Despite everything, I know in my heart you are the one. I'll take the good with the bad.

With that she climbed under her covers, closed her eyes and drifted into the first sound sleep she had had in a long time.

A sleep accompanied by dreams of the man she loves and all the ways they could show each other their love over the years to come. Her dreams started out peaceful and sweet but they quickly turned hot and sensual.

Nicolai pulled up to his house slowly. He parked in the drive way, turned off the car and sat staring at the steering wheel. He picked up his phone and looked at the messages Gilly had just sent him. Her last message made him want to cry.

It was taking all he had not to. She had said very little but what she said was the greatest thing he had ever read. He sat there, looking at the message over and over again, replaying the words in his head. It didn't take him long to realize he had a rough time ahead of him but the prize at the end was worth it.

He got out of the car and started to walk up the drive to the door when the hairs on his neck started to stand on edge. Something wasn't right.

He hurried to the front door only to stop in his tracks as he reached for the handle. He heard a noise to his side, he turned to face the dark and saw nothing but the depths of night. Muttering to himself about needing to leave the front light on he opened the door and went in.

He switched on the light inside the door and set his keys on the front hall table. He made his way into the kitchen to get a beer from the fridge, noticing the lack of food in the fridge. Shaking his head he turned only to drop the bottle when he came face to face with an unexpected guest. His first reaction was to take the fist he had formed at his side and slam it into the jaw of the man standing in front of him.

"Nicolai, I would reconsider that plan of attack if I were you." Neit could see what Nicolai was planning next and he had no intention of letting the young man get a swing in on him.

Nicolai was stopped on the spot. The man who just spokes voice was deep, powerful and thick with a Scottish brogue. The strange thing was he was calmed by the sound of it. There was strength and knowing in this man's voice. The only thing he couldn't figure out was how the man knew he was going to swing.

His fist had been clutched tight at his side, he hadn't raised it yet and Nicolai knew he didn't look like a man that would throw the first punch so he just wasn't sure what to think.

"Who are you?" Nicolai made it a demand not a question. He knew how to make himself intimidating and he planned on using it just to find out this man's next step.

"Shouldn't you have asked what I am doing here first?" Neit asked, a little curious as to the answer he would get.

"No, I asked the question I meant. If you were going to do me any harm you'd have done it by now. You would have made your move while I was distracted." Nicolai walked past the man in front of him towards the couch. He sat down, turned on the television, invited his strange guest over and went on with his night. He would get his answers, he could see that. He also saw that he was going to have a few more questions. He couldn't help but think that it was going to be a long night.

Neit looked at Nicolai and almost laughed. He was an arrogant man, no doubt about that. He was also surprisingly stubborn, just like Neit himself. He couldn't believe how he lucked into finding the young man. There was going to be a lot to discuss and many things to explain but he would play the boys games for the time being.

Chapter 9

Nicolai starred at his new found companion in amazement. They hadn't really talked the rest of the night last night, just simply sat in silence watching sports highlights and drinking a few beers.

The only words spoken were a quick good night and letting his guest know what rooms he could choose from to stay in. He then went to his room on the opposite side of the house where he fell asleep almost instantly and was haunted by tempting dreams of Gilly. When he woke up this morning in a sweat from his last dream he decided to go into the kitchen to try to find something for breakfast. He was amazed to see his still nameless house guest cooking a feast of bacon, eggs and biscuits.

He approached the counter where the food was laid out wondering what it was he had gotten himself into last night by allowing the man to stay.

"You know Nicolai; sometimes your thoughts are a little confusing."

BATTLING FOR LOVE

Nicolai looked at the man contemplating what he meant by that random statement.

Battling for Love

"I meant that I can't follow you sometimes. You are all over the place. Don't you ever just sit and clear your mind? It might help once in a while."

Nicolai was starting to feel like there was more going on here then he first expected...even though he wasn't sure of what he even thought at first. He needed to figure out exactly what this odd man was talking about.

He was reading his thoughts? Was that even possible? After all he had seen at Gilly's the night before he would believe anything. Then he thought a little more about the entire situation. Could this man here have something to do with

Maeve's being at Gillyanna's? Was he a threat or friend? Would he be an ally or enemy?

"Nicolai, slow down. I am getting lost on your thought train here. Give me a chance to catch up. The first thing is this…I don't appreciate being the 'odd' man. My name is Neit. Yes I am reading your thoughts but only because you aren't asking the questions aloud. I am here because of Maeve. I am the Celtic God of Battle.

I have been a friend of Maeve's for millennia and her confidant in battle. I am not a threat to you by any means. In fact I am here for your help and to help you. I am in love with Maeve and need to make her see what is between us and I need to help you and Gilly in order to help open Maeve's eyes to all there is."

Nicolai stood there staring. Holy fuck man…

"The other thing is Maeve doesn't know I am here, nor is she going to know. I will be tuned into her so that when she returns to her realm I will be waiting there for her. You have to keep my being here a secret."

Nicolai looked at Neit and thought about all he had said. He remembered Gilly mentioning the name of the God before him. He was greatly feared and adored all at once, a man of true power and character, a humane God, a man with great battle strategy and pose, a man of perfection.

The way Gilly had gone on about the man had made him a little jealous at the time but now he saw she was just speaking the truth. Then he thought…what could this God want with him?

"Ah, now you're thinking more clearly. To answer your last question as I was watching Maeve and the ladies she taken under her wing I also caught glimpses of you, including when they were dancing under the stars…" Nicolai flinched a little under the Gods stare, "however that is not what caught my eye. It was how much you are like me. I don't know if you are aware of this but there is a reason you accepted me so quickly. You are my son on Earth. You are my eyes, ears and work here on and in this realm."

Nicolai sat down, stared at Neit and then all of a sudden he knew all he said was true. He could feel it. It felt right in his heart. How is it that he could try to make Gilly walk away from something like this when it was clear that he is a part of this world as well. It also shows that there are more reasons for him and Gilly to be together.

Gilly being the daughter of the Goddess and him the son of the God, both incarnates to powerful beings, both together being strength and battle and passion.

"Okay, Neit. I am in. Whatever it takes to get us our women, I am in, Father." Nicolai smiled at Neit and nodded.

"Alright my son, first we work on us and I catch you up on what you need to know and be trained on as my incarnate. There are more questions to ask and answer but as we go along our trails we keep wooing our women. You have a foot in the door with Gilly, she loves you openly and she is going to give you a chance. I fear in all the year Maeve and I have been together we have never well...been together. In fact our first physical contact was a hug before she came here." Neit was a little tense and shifting a lot while waiting for Nicolai's response.

Nicolai looked at Neit and almost laughed. He didn't dare open his mouth out of fear of being disrespectful so he just thought to himself how funny the big bad God of Battle looked. How he was acting like a teenager caught up in his first love. Then he caught Neit's gaze and realized the God was reading his thoughts again.

"That's cheating a little don't you think? Am I not allowed a little privacy here?" He cracked a smile and chuckled as Neit just shook his head and went back to his cooking. Nicolai liked the idea of having the God of Battle on his side, at least now he knew he'd have the strength to overcome anything. It also meant that for the

first time in his life he would have a friend that knew everything about him and liked him for it.

He felt kind of foolish for thinking it but he was looking forward to a true friend. For once he wasn't just someone others turned to; to get ahead instead he was a companion…to a God no less.

"Li, I am not a super hero for crying out loud you're going on like a kid. Now grab a plate and eat up, big day ahead of us." Neit just laughed at the boy and thought the kid might have a point.

Chapter 10

Gilly was running as fast and hard as she could. She was barefoot, hair flowing behind her and her long skirt kissing her ankles while it danced in the wind. She was out of breath from laughing so hard. She turned her head to peer behind her, her smile grew larger and a fresh burst of laughter came from somewhere deep within.

Nicolai was right on her heals. She tried to break into a faster run but knew he would catch her sooner than later. He always did. These chases always start out the same; she was starting to think he let her have the head start just so he could give chase.

They had been lying in the clearing, their favorite spot in the world, deep in the woods behind Gillyanna's house. It was Gilly's refuge; she would go there to think, write, get away and just disappear when the world seemed to be too much.

She showed it to Nicolai their first year together. It was where they had first made love. It had been beautiful, starting with the softest, shyest of kisses and quickly turning into passion and fire, slowly their bodies ignited and moved together, touching and tasting all they could reach.

Gilly who was lost in this memory was quickly sucked back to the task before her, running fast, weaving between trees and laughing a husky, loud, brilliant laugh, by Nicolai's deep voice.

"Sweetling, where are you planning on running to?" Nicolai's voice was heavy with laughter and sounded even sexier than usual. There was strength and power in it but you could hear the humor too. He was seldom like this and Gilly planned on taking full advantage.

"Wouldn't you like to know? You're getting a little slow baby. You should have caught me by now." Her voice was breathy and light, the laughter in it almost too hard to control. She didn't know why she liked this game so much. Maybe it was the touch of childhood fun, the teasing, the way it always ended with her being caught and showered in his kisses. She didn't think she could pick out one reason. All of them were great reasons to keep running though.

Nicolai just laughed and kicked into high speed. He had let her take the lead long enough and although he liked watching her run from behind, her rounded, tight backside wiggling, her laughter lingering after she was gone, he couldn't take it anymore.

He needed her in his arms, her lips against his and her hips pressed firmly to his. Just the thought of it gave him the extra push he needed. Within moments Gilly was screaming with laughter as his arms wrapped around her waist and he swung her through the air.

She was swinging her arms and fighting his hold in feigned horror all while caught in a fit of laughs. This was Nicolai's second favorite part about the chase, the way her laughter filled the air and her smile lit up her face. It made him feel complete and whole. These were the few moments where he was the way he wanted to be with Gillyanna McFly, the way he wished things were all the time. He knew they could be but he had to get to that point first.

He had a lot to do before the world he belonged to would accept this side of him. "I caught you

Sweetling." It was just a simple statement accompanied by a big grin and hint of laughter but when Gilly looked in his eyes she saw that there was a cloud there. If she didn't act fast she would lose this moment, he would shut off again. She needed to keep him here with her for as long as she could. Her heart needed it.

"Yes honey, you did." Still laughing she lowered her mouth to his and caressed his lips with hers; slowing lifting her face from his she looked him right in the eyes. It had been a feather light touch, barely making contact.

Nicolai took in a deep breath and she grinned wide and proud. She took advantage of his distracted state and kissed him again this time she made it deep, sensual and slow.

She wrapped her arms around his neck and legs around his hips giving Nicolai the chance to let his hands roam. When he slid one hand into her hair to hold her head there as he took the kiss to new heights she moaned. Goddess she loved the way he kissed. His lips pressed hard against hers, his tongue stroking hers with the finesse of a swordsman. Their tongues would duel and caress in the most intimate ways. When his other hand slid up under her skirt she jerked a little from surprise but quickly welcomed the feel of his rough hands on her thighs and backside.

"Gilly, baby, I can't stand much longer." Nicolai spoke against her lips and she grinned again. The fact that he couldn't even pull away from her long enough to speak showed her the effect she had on him. She laughed into his mouth and held on tighter.

Nicolai groaned when she wrapped her body around his tighter grinding herself against his erection. She really knew how to drive him crazy. He had one hand in her thick wavy hair the other on her tight backside pulling her against him.

She was wiggling and moaning ever so slightly and he wanted to make her cry out. His legs were starting to give out on him and he decided to give into the urge to lay her down.

As slowly and carefully as he could he dropped to his knees and lowered her to the ground without breaking their kiss. He had her where he wanted her, pinned under his body where the only thing she could do was press her curves against him.

Gilly let out a groan as Nicolai lowered his body on top of her. She couldn't believe he had managed to get them to the ground without breaking their kiss. She was impressed and her blood was running hot. She could feel her heart beat in her toes. She wanted him. Here, Now and with all the fire that was heating her from the inside out. When he finally broke their kiss she voiced her displeasure with a groan only to choke on it as he started to kiss her collar bone and neck.

His hands were all over all at once. Moving up her sides, over her thighs, over her shoulders, in her hair, she wasn't sure where they would land next. The anticipation added to the feel of his rough skin against her softness had her panting.

When he finally stopped his roaming he did so to push her blouse up and over her head. He followed the action with his tongue tasting his way up her. He stopped to pay attention to her erect nipples and she let out a loud low moan of appreciation.

She could already feel the heat pooling in her stomach and she wondered just how long he would torment her before he gave her what she wanted. As he laved one nipple with his tongue encircling it and pulling it into his mouth to suck and nibble he used the other hand to caress the other. She arched into his palm, her nipple hardening even more in his touch.

Nicolai groaned and buried his head in Gilly's neck, taking in her smell. She smelt of wildflowers and the wind. He knew it was an odd thing to think but it was the truth. She smelt of women, softness and freedom. That's what she was to him. His freedom and he planned on running away with it for as long as he could.

He'd catch her breeze and let it carry him.

As he continued to tease her nipples with his mouth he let his hand slide slowly up her inner thigh. The way her breathing became labored with pants and moans had him going crazy; it took all of his control to not spill himself there. When he finally reached the center of her and touched her bud she bucked under his touch he growled.

She was wet and hot already. She wanted him, he could smell it on her and he didn't have the control to drag out the game anymore.

"Li, take me, now. I can't wait anymore. I need you in me."

Gilly wasn't surprised to hear how husky her voice was. She was surprised however by how hard it was to speak. She could barely think,

Nicolai's touch had her lost in thoughts and the world around them. Nicolai laughed breathlessly and just nodded against her neck where he had collapsed when she had spoken. He pulled

his hands away and she watched him as he undid his pants. Slowly he lifted up and stared down at her.

His eyes were almost black with passion. She loved how they could go from their normal blue and green to this dark sexy color. He lifted her skirt, slowly lowered himself down onto her, he teased her only a little and slid against her bud ready to slide into her moist heat…and just like that Gilly woke up in a panting sweat with a start. She didn't know what had disrupted her from her little slice of heaven but she wished she could fall back asleep.

It had felt so real. She was wet still and could almost smell the meadow around her and

Nicolai; she could still feel his hands on her aching nipples. Letting out a sigh of frustration she got out of bed and started to make her way to the kitchen. She was going to have to make a feast to clear her head enough to help her answer all the questions she had about her dream.

She would talk to Maeve about it and hope that she would have the answers she needed. Little did she know though but Nicolai woke the same way from the same sweet dream across town.

Chapter 11

Neit laughed out loud when he came into the kitchen this morning. The first thing he saw was Nicolai hunched over sulking and cursing under his breath. When Nicolai just looked at him and scowled Neit laughed harder and walked to the fridge. He was finding that Li kept him easily entertained when he was in a sour mood.

It helped ease a little of the tension he was holding because he knew today Maeve would return to her realm to meet with him and talk. He was looking forward to it but he was also anxious. He was going to make a move today. Well he was going to try. He wanted to push the boundaries with Maeve because he knew if he did she would break. He turned back to Nicolai to see the mans demeanor hadn't changed, he was going to just look inside his head to find out what was wrong but he had promised Nicolai his privacy so he just asked.

"Alright Son, what's got your balls in a bunch this morning?"

"If only you knew how right that statement was." Nicolai sat there and heaved a great sigh. He had woken up this morning in the worst mood thanks to an unfinished dream. He still couldn't believe the timing. In his dream he and

Gilly had been making love, well they had started to.

He was just about to join there bodies together when he woke up. It had felt so real that his body had responded even in his sleep. He woke up hard and ready only to be alone in his room and no Gilly. After a cold shower this morning his blood had cooled a little but he still wanted Gilly.

Neit had to bite his tongue. He had almost said something he was sure would result in Li throwing a punch or two his way. He could see the young man was suffering and judging from his comment it was probably from the same things he himself was.

"What's wrong my boy?"

"It's personal."

"Humph, well in that case I could just take a peak myself if you don't feel like sharing with the class." Neit really did enjoy pressing Nicolai's buttons.

"Okay fine. I had well this dream…it felt so real. I woke up at a really bad time and now I'm a little pissy okay?" Nicolai could see his answer wasn't enough for the God so he went into more detail.

"It was a dream about Gilly and I. Almost like a memory. It felt like she was there. I could smell her. I think we were together in this dream, no one person could dream something so real."

Neit looked at Nicolai in astonishment. The man had just described something that could only be defined as a shared dream. That meant that both Nicolai and Gilly had been calling to each other in their sleep. This was something he needed to look into. For now he would take in what the boy said and then make his way to Maeve.

"Li I think I know what you speak of but I need to look into it more because this could be the key to us breaking down some walls with our women. However for the time being I need to return to the realm Maeve and I share and speak with her. Forgive me for disappearing on you; you may want to find something to keep you busy. AH I know…why don't you go see your parents? Or Gilly?"

Nicolai watched the God vanish before his eyes and decided to get off his ass and start the day. His parents or Gilly? He wanted to go to Gilly and make the dream come true but he needed to talk to his parents. Today was looking to be a horrible day. He knew he would be doing the second hardest thing he had ever done in his life, the first was hurting Gilly.

No this would be almost as bad, he was telling his father and mother that he would no longer be a part of the family firm. He wasn't going to play into the politics and was no longer going to shape his life around the ideals of out dated old men. He was going to start his own practice and take Gillyanna, the smart mouth, wild, obnoxious, silly woman she was and marry her not because she was a good fit to keep up appearances but because he was madly, irrevocably and truly in love with the woman she was.

His parents were not going to take this well at all. He would just have to go in, stand his ground, and hope for their blessing. Worst case, they would tear him to pieces and he would feel defeated but at least he would finally be thinking for himself and living the life he has always wanted and he would finally be able to be the man he needed to be for Gilly. If all goes well they can be together sooner than later.

Nicolai stood up, smiled to himself and walked out the front door. He was ready for this, after all the God of Battle had taken him under his wing.

He was the God on earth. Time to face the battle head on and win.

Neit arrived back in the realm he and Maeve shared and looked around. It looked the same as when he left it but it didn't look like he had been living here the past week. He quickly went through straightening up a few things while messing up a few others.

He summoned some yellow roses and scattered them all over the living space they shared. He changed out of the jean and t - shirt attire he had come accustomed to while living at Nicolai's and put on well a little less. He grabbed a goblet of mead and lounged on the day bed facing the way Maeve would enter. He stretched himself out, flexed a few muscles and made sure that the little bit of cloth he was wearing covered just enough

to keep Maeve curious.

Chapter 12

He had just gotten comfortable when the first sign that Maeve had arrived hit him. He was quickly consumed by the smell of mead, roses and that little extra that was true to Maeve's natural fragrance.

His body started to grow taut with anticipation and he thought that it was a good thing that he was wearing so little because now Maeve wouldn't be able to ignore his desire even if she tried. He started sweating from nerves. There was a loud sound that reminded him much of the rigor of battle drums and Maeve was standing before him. She was the kind for theatrics at times.

He caught a glimpse of her but quickly looked off out the window, appearing to be distracted so that she wouldn't think he was waiting for her since she hadn't actually told him she was coming to the realm today.

Maeve had connected to the realm she and Neit had been sharing for the past few millennia and felt his presence instantly. She took her time appearing and used some over the top tricks to try to catch his attention. Silly as it was she was hoping to make him notice her. She let a breeze carry the smell of her throughout the realm in case he was off in some far corner and then let the battle drums rumble low and long.

She wanted him to hear her coming from every possible inch the realm covered…and it was a large realm. She let her little game go on for longer than it should have and then she finally let herself be seen but what she saw upon entering made her pause. Her entry way was covered in yellow roses. In fact the entire living area she shared with Neit was cover in yellow roses. She glanced around herself and everywhere she could see was a golden paradise. She scooped up a few into her arms, smelling them and taking in their attar.

She started to walk farther into the sitting room only to stop dead in her tracks and drop her flowers. Neit was on the settee in front of her in nothing but a piece of cloth covering his bronzed smooth skin. He was looking out the window like he hadn't even noticed her grand entrance.

While he was distracted she took the time to take him in. His muscles were taut and well defined from the position he was sitting in.

His chest broad and glistening with what she thought was sweat, but she didn't know why he would be sweating in here. He was holding a dazzling goblet in one hand while the other was positioned above his head in a very relaxed manner that stretched his form out longer tightening all the muscles in his chest and stomach. She lowered her gaze to the well-formed "V" shape at his hips. It was a sexy thing, like an arrow pointing to whatever glory the slim piece of fabric he wore covered.

Then she noticed exactly what that cloth covered. It was standing up like a marquee. He was hard with desire. She could see it and she let out a whimper of wanting. He looked every bit the strong, masculine God she knew he was.

It took all of his control not to turn and look at her when she finally came in. Everything about her was calling his attention but he had to play his cards right. He needed her to want him before he even acknowledged her, so while he looked out the window he kept thinking of the things he planned to do to her so that his desire and manhood stayed at full attention.

He could hear her moving around and he wanted to see what she was doing but he was determined to make her think he hadn't noticed her. When she let out a low, husky whimper he slowly turned his head toward her. He finally got a glance at her and what he saw almost made him jump up and take her then.

She was wearing a sheer white gown that hung loosely around her shoulders and was only dark enough to cover the most tempting areas. She looked amazingly like a Goddess, but of course she was one.

Slowly he rose from the settee letting the cloth slide a bit and reveal a little before he fully stood up. When her eyes caught his he just smiled. He knew he had her but now he wanted to see how far he could push her before she made a move or before he had to make one himself. He approached her slowly and handed her the goblet in his hand.

"You sound a little parched Maeve. I didn't expect you to come home today." He spoke barely above a whisper and moved around her in a circle as he spoke.

"Ye-s-s, I am. Thank you Neit." Maeve's voice was barely a whisper. Neit was so close she could smell him. She could smell desire and sex on him. If she didn't know any better she would think he was trying to seduce her.

She liked the idea of that so she decided to play along with it. Maybe she could push him a little further then he had anticipated for this little game. It would explain what he was up to. She could play the clueless maiden role for a while after all it could be fun.

"Why so quiet my Goddess?" Neit was pressing against her back, leaning over her shoulder to whisper in her ear. He liked calling her his; he could get used to it easily.

"Just taking it easy on my poor dry throat my warrior, wouldn't want to harm my voice."

Maeve spoke slowly and soft, letting the huskiness caused by his tender touches flow into her voice like honey. "You wouldn't want that would you?"

She pressed herself against him briefly as he moved behind her. When he let out a growl she knew she had guessed his game right, she liked this foreplay. What she hadn't anticipated was him grabbing her by the waist and pulling her against him tighter but she kept her initial shock under control and push back against him until her back side was against his hardness and her back against his chest.

She couldn't believe he was trying to seduce her but she wanted him so badly she didn't care; even if it was only lust she was going to take all he would give her.

Neit had realized that Maeve had caught on to him and he had expected her to ask questions but she didn't. He was going to start questioning her and find out why she was playing along. He wanted to know what she was thinking, what she was feeling, if she wanted him or just any man.

He started to ask and stopped himself because he was afraid the answer wouldn't be what he wanted to hear. His game backfired on him. He was now the one that was vulnerable, putty in Maeve's hands.

She could break him right now if she wanted to, he would do anything she asked of him. He was in trouble. Just where would she stop...would she stop? Right now she had him going so crazy he didn't think he could stop if they started. She was pressed against him, whispering in her husky voice just loud enough to hear and cause him to get the chills.

"Maeve…you have no idea what you're doing to me right now. This is a dangerous game." He spoke through gritted teeth.

"You started this game Neit. Do not place the blame on me. I accepted your challenge. Will you accept mine?" She could tell he was having trouble keeping control and wished he would just give in and stop torturing them both. She had never wanted any man the way she wanted him right now. This wasn't just a lust fueled passion; there was true emotion behind her...love. This would be the only way she could love him without telling him with words. She was still too afraid that he would reject her.

Neit turned her to face him, slid his hands slow up from her waist to her shoulders pausing slightly at her breast to caress them with his thumbs. She let out a gasp and sighs all at once.

Her reaction made him shiver. He looked her in the eyes and could see the desire clouding her pale blue eyes, darkening them faintly. She met his gaze with determination, the challenge in them clearly portrayed.

"You dare challenge the God of Battle?"

"Ha. As the Goddess of War yes I do challenge you. As the Goddess of Sexuality I beg you to make it good."

Neit's gaze never wavered from hers. He knew what she was asking and he was too far gone for him to deny her.

This is what he wanted. He asked for this and now he would get it.

"This is one battle I don't mind losing loving. I gladly throw in the white flag." And with that he lowered his mouth to hers and firmly kissed her. Their lips melted together, moving in perfect harmony. He nipped at her bottom lip and when she gasped he slid his tongue into her mouth and explored the sweet taste of her. She met his actions move for move, their passion building with each passing.

Maeve thought she had heard him call her loving but words of endearment whispered through lust powered lips held no meaning. She couldn't let her heart race over nothing. She wanted it to be real. She wanted him to mean it. Her heart wanted it, no her heart needed it. She couldn't trust these words though. She would have to let her heart speak through her actions and hope that he would start to feel the same way. She didn't want this to be the only time so she would do anything she had to, to make it happen again even if it meant giving up some of her pride to do so. Her pride was her worst enemy as it were.

She was lost in her thoughts and the feeling of Neit's hands moving against her body, his lips moving against hers and the feelings engulfing her and it felt like magic. It was nothing she had ever felt before. She had felt lust but this was so much more. She had never been in love with any of her consorts or husbands. Neit was the only man to hold her heart; he was also the only person close to her that didn't know it. She wanted to tell him, she wasn't sure how long she could keep it in.

She was afraid she wouldn't be able to. That it would slip out. She just had to hope that he would think it was just words muttered out of lust if he heard them. She had to pull herself from her own thoughts and pay attention to what was being done to her. It didn't take much to do that though because Neit's kisses had moved to her collar bone as he pressed her up against the wall, using his body to pin her there as he devoured her. She was moaning and panting out of control. She was getting louder by the second. She clutched at him, clawing his shoulders and back.

Neit let out a feral growl when she dug her nails into him. The way she was clutching at him had him wanting her more. She was so responsive to every touch. Every little move brought a sound of enjoyment from her that equaled his. He was finding it hard to keep control. He wanted her so much. Hard, fast and now but he wanted to do this right. He wanted this to be something she never forgot.

He took his hands and slid them up her sides taking the blouse she was wearing with them. He paused only slightly when he reached her breasts so that he could tease the tender flesh there. He only removed his lips from hers to lift off her shirt the last bit only to return his lips to hers and kiss his way down to her breast. He held on to his last strand of control when Maeve bucked in his arms as he ran his tongue over her nipple.

Maeve couldn't believe how badly she was wriggling and gasping under Neit's strong hands. He was driving her crazy. She almost lost all sense of control when his tongue lashed out over her already sensitive nipple. When he took it in his mouth she couldn't take it anymore. She let out a scream of pure pleasure. She was begging him to end the torture. She didn't care if she lost this round; she planned on having a few more before she departed back to earth. She could win those.

"Neit, by the Gods! Please, please stop torturing me. I need you now." Neit almost lost complete control when she said that. He was already finding it hard to stand up and keep this teasing going. He decided then to make it a little easier.

He kissed Maeve good and hard and then swept her up in his arms. When she laughed breathlessly against his lips he grinned. He pulled away, gave her a peck on the nose and carried her over to the settee. He set her down and lowered himself on top of the Goddess.

Maeve loved that he had this little touch of playfulness. It was cute. It also showed her how much he cared and that they could be themselves around each other. That wasn't something she was worried about though. They had always had a sense of comfort with each other. He was her best friend. That last thought made her little train of happiness come to a halt. He was her best friend. Would what they were doing change that? Would she lose this friend she had come to need?

She wanted this with him but she couldn't lose this friendship. Sometimes Neit was the only thing that kept her going.

Neit looked down on her and could see a dark cloud in her beautiful eyes. They really were stunning but he was shaken by the sadness he was seeing now. What had he done wrong? The look in her eyes had been like a splash of cold water to his face. He wanted this more than anything and he wanted her. He needed her. He loved her more than she could even know.

He didn't want to stop what they had started but he needed to know why she looked like someone had taken away all the sunshine.

"Maeve, love, what has chilled you so?"

"I don't feel chilled do I?" She tried to give him a playful smile to cover up the sadness in her voice but she could tell her didn't believe it for a moment. She looked into his molten eyes and saw all the fire and passion there but now there was a touch of tenderness and worry. His whole body was tense but not as it had been before.

This tension could only be from uneasiness.

She decided she should tell him what was on her mind. She had never held back before now so she wouldn't keep it in this time either.

"I am scared." She spoke barely above a whisper and wouldn't meet his gaze. She felt defeated. She just wanted him to go back to driving her so crazy she couldn't think.

She finally looked back and him and thought that maybe she could start doing a little touching and get the ball on the roll again. Maeve let her hand role over his hip and along his backside slowly, caressing ever so lightly.

"What has you so frightened my dear goddess?" Neit had to ask in a murmur. The way her fingers were dancing over him was starting to heat his blood once again. He had been hurt when she wouldn't look at him and slightly amused by how pitiful she looked when admitting weakness.

"You do. I want you so badly I can't think clearly and yet I am so afraid of crossing this line and losing your friendship. I need you in more ways than you know." She spoke in a sultry tone, deep and husky like she was sharing a precious gift through those few words. She was though, she hadn't said the words exactly but she had just offered him her heart. How he took this would determine her next move. The whole time she let her hands roam from his back to chest in a teasing manor.

Neit stared down at her, he really looked at her. In her eyes was fear, lust, compassion and there was that something he really wanted to believe was there. Her voice had him trapped. He couldn't turn back now.

"My sweet Honey Mead, you will never lose me. No matter the battle, the troubles, moments of insecurity and loss, I am here for you always love." With that he lowered his head back down and met her lips with his. He kissed her so tenderly and calmly, trying so hard to keep the beast of passion under control till she was ready for it.

Maeve responded to his kisses with a sigh. He was right. He had always been there and she knew he would be. The way he had spoken to her had been enough for her to let down her guard and give him her whole heart, even if he

didn't know it…yet. She gave herself over to him; body, heart and soul in that moment.

Neit could feel her relax in his arms. He finally felt all of her at once, she had given herself to him and he knew what that meant, whether she had voiced it or not he had won her heart. He finally had Maeve. The battle wasn't over yet but he was that much closer to his victory. He kissed her as deeply and passionately as he ever had.

When Maeve reached between him and removed the almost nonexistent piece of cloth he wore and wrapped her hand around his length Neit had to grit his teeth to stop himself from spilling his seed right then. He looked her in the eyes as he returned her touch. He slowly slid his hand down her stomach and touched her core.

He found her wet and ready. He stroked her a few times and then carefully moved her hand away from his manhood. He kissed her again this time meeting the thrust of her tongue with the trust of his hips. He entered her slowly and deeply.

He made his movements gentle and caught her moans in his mouth. He wanted to go faster but he also wanted to make this moment last as long as he could. When Maeve wrapped her legs around him pulling him deeper into her he moaned and quickened his thrusts. He was dangerously close to release but he wasn't going to take it until she was ready for hers.

As he thrust into her he slide his hand over her shoulder, down her arm, clasped her breast and lowered his mouth to it. He teased her nipple with his tongue and lips. He kept sliding his hand down while he kept her distracted with his mouth. She was moaning and wriggling and met him thrust for thrust. She kept her hips in time with his, tightening and shifting around him. When his fingers found her bud she bucked against him, tightening herself dangerously around his already engorged member.

He caressed her quickly matching his hips with his fingers until she was gasping, panting and begging for release along with him. She clutched at his shoulders and pressed herself against him firmly and cried out his name as her release exploded around him. He found his as the last of his name fell from her lips. He plunged into her one last time, hard and deep, as he spilt his seed crying out "My Maeve" as he did.

Neit collapsed onto Maeve making sure he shifted his weight so not to crush her. He looked at her and kissed her slowly. He fell to the side of her pulling her half on top of him. He brushed her hair to the side and rested his chin on her head. She was still breathless but gave a content sigh when he wrapped his arms around her. As the lay their cuddling he started to drift off to sleep.

Maeve felt Neit's breath become steady and his body go limp, she looked up at him. He had his eyes closed and a manly smirk on his lips. She had heard him call her his when he found his release. She hated to admit it but that dominate manly act made her feel special and well…she liked it. She smiled up at him and chuckled a little to herself at the way he fell asleep. She could get use to this.

Making love to him, laying in his arms and falling peacefully to sleep.

"I love you Neit." She spoke in the softest whisper even though he was asleep. She didn't want to wake him or chance him hearing her.

She was still too afraid to say it out loud. She looked at him so peacefully laying there wishing she could spill her heart out to him right then to take the weight and worry off her chest. To just find out what he felt and find relief but she didn't. She held her tongue, lowered her head and drifted off to sleep.

Once Neit felt her body lax he risked opening his eyes. When she had first said "I love you" he almost let out a cheer! He couldn't believe it but he knew she only said it because she thought he

didn't hear. Now he knew…he just needed to
talk to Nicolai to see what to do next.

Chapter 13

Gilly hung up with Izett and started to get her things together. Izett decided to call another girls day but this time they would be taking Maeve with them, the Goddess was in need of some earthly clothing and human contact.

If she was going to be staying with them for a goddess only knows how long she would need to know how to fit in. Gilly was really looking forward to time with the girls. She set down her phone and went into the kitchen to clean up the last of her mess from the morning of cooking to clear her head. Her mind instantly went back to Nicolai and a smile formed on her face. She was glad they were on the road to recovery because now she could focus on Maeve, the Goddess had confided in her about Neit and now she knew why Maeve wanted her help.

The Goddess didn't know how to let her emotions show and she was afraid that if she told him that she loved him he would run from her. Ironically Maeve was a lot like Nicolai in that sense. Maeve had gone back to her realm to see

Neit last night and hadn't returned so Gilly was hoping that was a good sign.

"Maeve can you hear me?" Gilly felt silly looking upward talking into empty space.

Good morning child. I take it you slept well.

Gilly laughed. When she got up to find Maeve this morning the goddess had already returned to her realm so she had sent a long ranting message about the dream to the goddess while she was cooking this morning. A really pissed off, sexually frustrated, annoyed message to Maeve and all the goddess had said in return was "*It's called a shared dream daughter, if it makes you feel better he is suffering too.*"

The funny thing, knowing that Nicolai had felt all she had and that they had connected like that did make the tension disappear.

"Very funny Maeve, are you still joining Izett and myself today or are you going to lie in bed with that bronzed God all day?" Gilly couldn't help that one. She knew Maeve well enough to know that the goddess had gotten a little more than a talk last night otherwise she

would have been sulking in the kitchen with Gilly both grumbling over their men and lack of attention.

I knew you were smart Gillyanna. Yes I have too much to tell you today to not show up! However, I am still indispose and wrapped up in bronzed arms so I will just pop into the car when I am presentable. He hasn't woken yet and I am

enjoying this far too much.

Gilly grinned happy that at least one of them had fantasies being fulfilled. As she stood there lost in her thoughts her phone chirped and pulled her right out of a fantasy that was unfolding. She heaved a heavy sigh and opened her messages. It was a text from Nicolai and she burst into a silly smile.

So Sweetling, any interesting dreams last night?

She was taken back a little. How could he know? From what Maeve had told her of shared dreams they were an ancient thing tied to the Gods and were only shared when both people were connected to a God or Goddess.

Was it possible Nicolai was? But what God? Since when? Or was this all simply his ego hoping that she had dreamed of him?

Should I have?

She was hoping to lure him into answering one of her questions. She also sent Maeve her thoughts on it. Something was off.

I agree Gilly; I will do some probing too. Maybe Neit will know of a God that could be affiliated with your Boy-o. Wait...Neit...I think it's time to get out of bed and get some answers out of this bronzed beauty.

Gilly was really intrigued by this. Nicolai was tied to a God? How was that possible? It was obviously possible seeing as how she was tied to a Goddess but would that mean that she and Nicolai were drawn together on their own or because of some divine reasoning? Or was it because they are both divine that they are to be together?

"Maeve! What do I do?" Gilly was so confused.

I think we are both missing out on a little information from our men. It would seem that Neit has some explaining to do just as Nicolai still owes you some explaining.

"You don't think that Li is Neit's incarnate do you?" Gilly could barely wrap her head around the idea. Had he been lying to her this whole time? How could he have made her doubt in Maeve if he himself was connected to a God?

I most certainly do think that. It would make sense as to why Neit knew I'd return today. We talked here and there while resting through the night and he said some things to me that had me wondering about why he knows so much about you and Nicolai. How he knew I'd return today. Why you and Nicolai are destined to be. It explains so much about Nicolai himself. He holds many of the qualities that Neit does that I should have noticed sooner.

"That would also explain why we had the shared dream wouldn't it? Or how Li knows about it?"

Exactly! I have a feeling Neit has not only been watching over me but has been here along with me on Earth. Maybe you can make a visit to Nicolai?

"Today he with his parents clearing up something, it is part of his journey to fixing us…"

We will talk when I return. I have a feeling that a bottle…or bucket of mead will be needed for us both this evening. See you out on the town daughter.

"Alright Goddess, see you then."

Oh and call Izett. I already filed her in on this one. She will help you come up with a plan to get the guys to speak.

"Okay Maeve. Although I think she beat me to it, the phones ringing now."

Gilly answered the phone trying to focus while the Goddess's laughter echoed through her head, it is a contagious sound and it was almost impossible to control once she said picked up the phone and said hello.

"Let's get those boy-o's by the balls!" Izett's laughter had Gilly fall into a new fit of titters.

"So I take it you are on your way here then Izz?"

"Why Gillyanna, you should know I am already at the door."

Just then the doorbell chimed, Gilly hung up and opened the front door to see Izett standing there, wine in one hand, a bag of groceries in the other and a smile that lite up her face with pure trouble.

"Alright, let the planning begin!" Gilly grabbed the wine, locked arms with Izz and made her way to the kitchen.

Gilly started to go through the groceries to see what Izett had gotten for what was to be a girls night in now, a devious girls night in at that. She loved how close she was to these women and how much she needed them. She always felt like Izett was a sister but now that she knew they really were connected through the Goddess she felt closer to her than ever.

Not to mention only a truly wonderful friend would show up with wine and a bag of food for someone else to cook up and expect it to be a welcome gift. Luckily cooking was one way for Gillyanna to brainstorm. For some they need to run or drive around. For Gillyanna so needed to whip up a gourmet meal and let her mind wander. Izett knew her all too well.

Chapter 14

Izett and Gilly had spent the next hour talking, laughing and devising a plan to get the men to talk. They of course had decided that sex would be their weapon…it really was the only option.

Gilly had told Izett everything in the past hour, all the stuff she was afraid Izz couldn't accept and wouldn't support came out so that nothing was missing. Izett took it all really well her only criticism was that Gilly shouldn't have kept any of it from her in the first place. Izett had always been supportive of Gilly even if she wasn't a fan of the idea. After their heart to heart they popped open a bottle of wine, shared a glass and Gilly started to cook up dinner.

Gilly was a writer first and foremost and writing had always let her get out what she felt inside but cooking, cooking was a passion. Writing let her get her thoughts on paper, her ideas and imagination took on a life of their own.

Cooking? Cooking let her open her mind and take things in. It let her think and plan.

She had started cooking in her Grandmothers kitchen at a young age and even studied culinary arts while in college. Cooking cleared her head and opened her eyes to things she didn't see at first. It was an art form, a balance of flavor, technique, texture and presentation.

When she was done cooking she plated up for Izett, Maeve and herself. She laid out the table and Izett had just started eating when Maeve showed up. She entered the room in her normal dramatic fashion, her all eyes on me, hail me way of carrying herself and sat down with them easing her way into the conversation. It all felt so natural. The three of them together, talking, eating and laughing.

The connection was so strong it couldn't be ignored. They were more like best friends, sisters and confidants then a Goddess, her incarnate, and her daughter by divinity.

After a while Maeve brought up the men and asked what the girls had come up with to use as a way of getting information. Gilly couldn't help thinking that they were like Charlie's Angels or something. Super sneaky, devious, sexy spy woman. The idea was silly but seemed relevant to the situation they were in.

"So my lovely girls, what is our plan of attack?" Maeve looked from Gilly to Izett and laughed when she saw the spark in their eyes.

"Sex." Gilly and Izett said it in unison and loudly. Both very proud of the answer they had given to the Goddess. After all Maeve represented sexuality. They were merely walking with their best foot forward.

"Sex? Hmm…I like the idea but can you tell me more?"

"Well it was rather simple to come up with. We need information and your guys have it." Izett said with confidence. "You already said Neit had said some things to you last night between rounds so now all it will take is driving him mad with pleasure and asking the right questions."

"Yes, I can see how that would work but what about Nicolai? He doesn't have loose lips like the God." Maeve said this and already suspecting she knew the answer looked at Gilly and waited to hear what would happen.

Gilly took a deep breath and started to explain what would happen to get Nicolai to be as open with what he knew as the God was.

"Well it won't be as easily done on my end but we decided that we should use the shared dreams to start with. It is no surprise to any of us that Nicolai and I are both suffering from tension and since I don't have physical contact with him yet this is the first phase." Gilly explained. "I will call to him in my sleep and control the dream, now that we know how to do so with your help. I will torment him until he begs to see me and then once in person I will do the same until he is in a stupor and spills his guts."

"An excellent plan ladies! I think it is perfect. So we start tonight then?"

"YES!"

"I would like to point out that since you both will be getting a little it may be time to dip into the God pool and fish me out a hunk…what do you say? I am starting to run low on DD batteries and would really like to save a trip to the store." Izett said in all seriousness mid bite as she waved her hand through the air.

Maeve and Gilly burst into amusement. The funny thing about it was how serious Izett looked. Maybe when this was all done they could set her on her path with a man, after all she had been helping them with theirs. Maeve thought she just might know the perfect man for Izett but kept that thought to herself for the time being. After all she already told Izett that she had a plan for her. Who's to say that it won't involve a little romance?

"Izett, you can't go casually making comments like that!" Gilly was rolling with laughter but could see the look of longing in her best friends eyes and realized that no matter what it would take she would make sure Izett found happiness in the end.

"Yeah, yeah I am hilarious." Izett said waving her hands around and laughing with her friends.

"Now to really get into the details, Gillyanna you will need to take complete control of the dreams if this is to work. Do not let him know that you are aware of the dreams. The guys obviously think they are the only ones clued into them.

Also you cannot, under any circumstances let him take control. If he gets control of the dreams you will be the one begging in the end...not him"

"You're right. I need to stay strong and not give into my own desires. I have to be the one in control if we are to get any answers. Do you think he will talk?" Gilly was not so sure she could keep up the charade. She didn't have the sex appeal that Maeve had. She also wasn't sure she had the connection to Nicolai that Maeve has with Neit.

BATTLING FOR LOVE

"YES!" Maeve and Izett spoke in unison this time, both having all the confidence in the universe in Gilly.

"Gilly you are my incarnate, the incarnate of the Goddess of War, Intoxication, Personal power and SEX. Trust me, you can do this. Tap into the inner part of you where you keep me .This is a battle. Your instincts will kick in and when it comes to driving him mad with passion well lass, you will find no problem there."

Gilly stood a little taller after Maeve spoke. She had this. She just needed to believe in herself. It was time to see how much she had acquired from the Goddess.

"Well ladies…I think it's time for drinks and a little fun and then calling it an early night!" Izett said as she took a drink directly from the bottle of liquor. All three women laughed and started an early celebration of their soon to be victory over the men.

Gilly kept a little sadness in her heart. She was so afraid of opening up to him. She wasn't sure she really had the strength for this again. It would break her completely if Nicolai didn't come around this time.

She loved him, she would continue to love him but her heart was breaking a little more every time she had to live in the fear of him not coming back to her. He was worth the pain no questions asked. She just had to have faith…it was easier said than done at this point though.

She whispered her doubts to Maeve and then something caught Gilly by surprise; a single yellow rose tattoo appeared on Gilly's wrist. It was painless but sent warmth through her. She gasped and looked at the Goddess.

"The yellow rose carries many meanings now days. At one time it was negative. It was a symbol of dying love. This is no longer the case. A yellow rose given by me means joy, wisdom and power. You now carry my rose with you everywhere you go. Let the power fill you, let the joy chase away your sadness and let the wisdom be your guide to love."

Gilly smiled through the tears and threw herself into the Goddess's arms. Izett was quickly by their side to join in on the embrace. The women stood there a moment until Gilly's stomach growled making them all laugh.

"Okay, pity party over, back to celebrating. Someone give me a damn food and let's get this going!" Gilly laughed at herself truly enjoying the way life was playing out for the first time in a long time.

Chapter 15

Nicolai looked from his mother to his father and back again. They both just stared at him like he was unreasonable. He had to admit though that this was going better than he planned. They had agreed to lunch, they let him get all he had to say out and now they were processing it all...or at least he thought they were.

He was a little surprised that his dad hadn't ripped him apart yet. He thought for sure that when his father, Ian, had heard him say he was leaving the firm he would have exploded after all Nicolai working for the firm his father ran had been his father's idea as well. He was lost in these thoughts waiting for something to happen, waiting for his father to turn red in the face and unleash his wrath.

Waiting for his mother to cry and say he was throwing everything away. His mother, Nessa, was the one to finally break the silent standstill they were trapped in. She reached across the table, gave his hand a squeeze, and smiled meekly at him.

"You will not be leaving the firm. If you love the girl this much then that is enough for us. I have never seen you show such passion before. That is what makes a good man." Nessa's words held no bitterness, anger or judgment. She spoke softly with affection and pride. Her Irish drawl flushing over him like a cool comfort. Nicolai found it oddly ironic.

He was taken back to a time when he was younger and told his mom he didn't want to be a lawyer. She had spoken to him the same way she did now. She had said one day he would be challenged and a secret that he would find out when he was a grown man would be the key to his victory.

She said there was a destiny to him…wait did she know about Neit? She then told him the significance behind her name. The original Nessa was the mother of a king. She was beautiful, powerful and had all the spirit the universe could offer. She made her son king. His father's name, Ian, meant God is forgiving. Hopefully his father could be as forgiving as his name suggested.

"Your Ma is right. It took you far too long to figure out what you wanted but now that you have there is no way you will be forced to give up anything you have achieved. How much faith were you lacking in us to think we would force you to be something you aren't? That we would make you try to change that girl? Change yourself? We told you, you needed to be rid of her so that you would defy us. That you would take a stand and tell us no you would not go along with it. You have never been eager to please and I needed to know that you could be

strong on your own." Ian stared down his son
waiting for him to absorb all that was said.

When Nicolai's face went from a twisted
confusion to understanding and then to defeat Ian
realized that Nicolai finally understood it all.

"You mean to tell me, I made the situation what
it is. I made things bad, no worse, all on my
own?"

"Yes boy-o. You had the chance at perfection; it
just took you too long to figure it out." Nessa felt

a pain deep inside for her son. He was aching.

She didn't like this at all. They knew the risk they were taking when they set forth on this task. A task the Dagda had given them many years ago. Unfortunately they couldn't change how it had to be done.

She was flooded with memories from when she was still young, barely halfway through her pregnancy with Nicolai. One night in particular stood out. She and Ian had been lying in bed talking about names for the baby. They couldn't decide on a name that would suit a child of theirs

BRANDI BALDESI

but Nessa had been pulled into a state of exhaustion before they could agree on one.

They had decided to sleep on it and pick up the conversation the next morning. They had plenty of time to decide. She had drifted into the deepest sleep she had ever had and lulled into a dream that was so realistic she could feel her hair rustled by the wind. In her dream she had been sitting by a fountain in the middle of a clearing in woods she had never before seen. There was something beautiful and serene about the place.

It felt like there wasn't a care in the world, nothing bad could happen to her there.

As she sat there staring at the water a face appeared next to her. But even in her sleep she did not jump or scare. She simply turned and smiled up at the man behind her, the Father of the Gods, Dagda.

"Hello, Dagda. It is good to see you Great Father."

"Hello Nessa. How are ye and the bairn today my daughter?"

"Well. You have blessed Ian and me with a healthy son. I am ever grateful. The only thing we seem to be having trouble on is a name to suit the babe."

"Ah my dear devoted child. That is why I have brought ye to the grove. I have much to tell ye this night."

"Is there something amiss with my bairn?"

"No Nessa. The child you carry has a destiny about him. There is much ye should know about him. He will be strong, a great protector. He is Nicolai."

"Nicolai? He is to be a Nicolai?"

"Yes. He will also be the incarnate of the God of Battle Neit."

Nessa put her hands on her stomach and swaddled the babe inside of her. Nicolai...the great protector. He was to be an incarnate of

Neit, the great God of Battle. She could feel the
pride and praise rising within her chest.

She started to weep tears of joy. She was pulled
from her thoughts when Dagda spoke again.

"There is more Nessa. There is a girl. She will be
born to another family of my followers in a few
years. She will be the woman your Nicolai loves.
Her name is Gillyanna McFly. She will be the
equal to your son. She is the incarnate of the
Goddess Maeve."

BATTLING FOR LOVE

"The Goddess of War, Sex and Intoxication? The great Goddess of Personal Power?"

"Yes. I see you remember your studies. Gillyanna will be the only one your son can love fully, equally and she will keep him happy all of his days."

"Is it to be that easy Dagda? That my son will be blessed with this great love?"

"No."

Nessa looked at Dagda in confusion. She wasn't sure what was going on but she had a feeling the next thing he was going to say would not make her happy.

"He will have to go through a trial. He will have to earn the love of Gillyanna. You and Ian will have to be the one to do this. When the time comes your son will need to feel that he has to choose, the career and future he believes you two want for him or a life with Gillyanna.

He will mess up. He needs to find her, push her away, lose her and then win her back. He will need to be tested so that he can prove he has the strength the God Neit needs of him. Neit will come to him in time as well. Just as Gillyanna will have the same choices, trials and struggles with the Goddess Maeve."

"Why must these children do this?" Nessa understood and she would do anything the God asked of her.

"In order to deserve one another, to deserve the future I have seen for them, in order to be incarnates that the gods need, they have to prove it." With that the Dagda kissed Nessa's forehead, placed a hand on her stomach and blessed his future son. The dream ended and Nessa woke to Ian looking at her.

"I know loving, all will be well. Our son is blessed by the Father God after all."

Nessa smile, curled up into her husband's arms and both of them fell into an undisturbed sleep.

"Ma? Are you okay?"

It was Nicolai's voice that pulled her back from her daydream.

"Yes. I was thinking about your destiny. The one the Dagda had told us long ago. If you are coming to us now it means that you have met Neit and are finally ready. Son, start your own life. Do not worry about doing what will make anyone but you and Gillyanna happy. You are ready for the task the Dagda appointed you with all those years ago."

"But what must I do mother?"

"First, go to your Gilly, make everything right with her. Then go from there boy-o." Nicolai looked at his mother and smiled. He then turned to his father to see him staring at Nicolai and smiling himself.

"I am proud of you. We are sorry things had to work out like this but this is what the Dagda asked of us. Go son. Be happy. We send our love with you"

Chapter 16

After Maeve returned to her realm to meet with Neit and carry out her part of the plan Izett and Gilly retired to the living room to relax. Izett had stayed to calm Gilly down a bit more. Gilly was too awake and anxious to even consider falling asleep.

She was stuck between nervous and excited. For the first time in a long time she would have Nicolai exactly as she wanted, granted it was only in sleep for now. She was hoping she could do a good enough showing so that she could make him want her so badly she wouldn't have to wait too long for him to be calling her begging to see her. She needed to get a hold of him first and make sure that he was thinking about her before bed. Plus she had to find out when Nicolai would be home and in bed.

"Gilly, just text him, it's not that hard. Flirt through text. Imagine it's just the same old playful banter you use to have with him before you guys were officially together." Izett looked

Gillyanna straight in the eye and handed her, her cell phone.

Gilly took her phone from Izett and scrolled to Nicolai's number in her contacts. She started a new message and sent it…beginning their plan.

I have been thinking about you all day Li

Nicolai responded almost instantly. Gilly couldn't help but think that this may be easier than she had originally thought.

Oh? Have you now baby?

She knew she had him right where she wanted him.

Yes. I have.

She wanted to keep him thinking, let his mind wander and make him curious all at once.

What have you been thinking?

Ha! She knew he would ask. Now the games would begin.

I've been thinking that it's been far too long since you have kissed me.

Hey…she had to keep it tame at first. These things needed to be built up to. Besides it had been a while since she had last proposition a man in a text.

I couldn't agree more loving. Is that all you were thinking?

Man if she didn't know any better he was setting her up for this one. She may have underestimated how badly he wanted her too. She might not need to do too much to make him call to her in his sleep.

Well...the kissing definitely turned in more. To be honest I may have blushed a little bit at the time. Once I started picturing all the things you could do to me with your hands, tongue and lips I was glad I was home alone.

She did a little bit of a happy dance after that one. Bouncing on the balls of her feet and spinning around.

Gilly if you're not careful this conversation may turn into more than simple texting.

BINGO! Gilly-1, Nicolai-0.

Actually Li, I am pretty tired now. I am going to call it a night. Sweet Dreams, maybe if you think about me hard enough you'll see me in yours.

Always leave them wanting more she thought to herself.

It's a date loving.

If only he knew what he was going to be getting once he drifted into their dream date. He wouldn't know what hit him but Gilly knew that if she could do everything right Nicolai would be knocking on her door ready to spill all his little secrets.

And with that Gilly grinned at Izett and made her way up to her room. It was time to see just how much of a woman she could be. Once she reached her bedroom she was weighted down by pressure. She needed to make sure Nicolai was the first one to sleep so she could slip into his

dream. Secondly, she had to decide exactly how she wanted to go about this. They had come up with a general idea but the little details needed to be done by her. After racking her brain for a little too long she decided she would go with the flow. She could manipulate his dream any way she wanted to.

So why not see what he was starting? She only had to remember to stay in control the whole time. He needed to be the one to beg.

Of course all of this didn't really matter.

Eventually they would both know all the truths. This was just more of an act of pride. Of proving her strength as a woman and finding out the truth through her connection to the Goddess.

She and Maeve might also be taking the secrets that the men they love are keeping a little personal. They wanted the guys to be completely open and honest with them yet they have both been keeping something so important hidden. It didn't help that Maeve and Gilly were both scarred from the past. Both terrified that these men who could so easily wound them might just do it. Might betray their hearts and use their weaknesses against them. Maeve said it was part of the warrior women inside of them that made them so weary. It was instinct to protect themselves from pain, even from heartache.

Gilly had never really noticed the things she had in common with the Goddess until she had spent more time with her. Maeve told her that had she been around as she grew up Gilly would have always noticed that she was a woman who held the same gifts as the Goddess, her own woman with her own thoughts but with the power and strength of a Goddess. Now that Maeve was around those strengths and powers would grow and develop.

She quickly showered, her favorite part of the house outside of her little writing corner was the master bathroom connected to her bedroom with its Jacuzzi style bath and rain top shower. She let the water roll over her and caress her skin. Every drop enhanced by her need to feel and the excitement gathering in her belly. Once she was relaxed she climbed into bed, turn off her lamp and slowly drifted into sleep, calling to Nicolai's sleeping mind the whole time.

It didn't take long before she had joined him in his dream, it was also clear he had gone to bed thinking of her. She was back in their clearing. It looked so much different compared to just a few

nights ago when she had summoned
the Goddess.

A beautiful blanket lay out with a spread of
finger foods. Grapes, strawberries, breads,
cheeses, an array of veggies and a glass of
wine were all lying before her. He really had
meant it would be a date.

Now however was when he would lose control
of this dream, but until she had the information
she needed he would have to think that the
changes had come from his mind not hers. If he

caught on too soon to her knowing about the shared dreams and learned that she knew enough about them to control them then she would be the one answering questions, not him.

When Nicolai stepped up behind her dream self and kissed the hollow of her neck she was drawn back to the dream and away from her wandering mind. It was time to take control.

Chapter 17

Nicolai had just fallen asleep when he was drawn into a dream and even though he couldn't sense her yet he knew it would be a shared dream with Gilly. He really liked this shared dreams thing. He decided to take some time and make the dream what he wanted.

He set them in their clearing. A picnic lay before them with all kinds of foods he could tease her with. Her favorite bottle of wine sitting there waiting for her. He sat there smiling with pride at what he had made for them. She was going to be putty in his hands.

He was sitting there thinking about her when he felt her presence join the sleeping realm. He quickly stepped into the shadows of the woods.

He didn't want her to see him yet. He wanted her to see what he had created first. He was going to sneak up on her. Let her think this was just her dream, not their dream.

When Gilly finally appeared in the dream realm sHe was facing the picnic, her back to Nicolai. She stood there awhile taking it all in. He really had surprised her with this one. He snuck up behind her, wrapped his arms around her and kissed the hollow of her neck. She didn't tense when he first made contact. Instead she arched into him and let out a sigh.

"You are here." Nicolai couldn't believe how good it felt to hold her. Shared dreams felt so real, it felt like she was really there.

"I told you if you thought hard enough about me I would be." Gilly loved the touch of him. How he was holding her made her so safe and warm.

"You did, and so I did. I haven't stopped thinking of you baby. You're all I think about."

He turned her then and kissed her. It was a deep; toe curling kissing that left them both panting when he finally pulled away. "I have something to tell you."

Gilly looked into his eyes and saw something she never would have thought. There was love. It wasn't clouded, there was no anger or hurt left to take away the pure, good love. For the first time she couldn't deny it.

"What did you want to tell me my love?" She smiled up at him hoping he would not hold anything back. She was going to indulge in this moment for as long as she could.

Nicolai saw the love radiating off of Gilly. He could also see the way her face lit up when she looked into his eyes and he knew for the first time she could honestly see he returned her feelings. He basked in the way she looked at him, taking it all in and remember the look she wore with hopes that his news to her would only brighten her eyes and smile more.

"Well baby, I spoke with my parents this morning." He was hoping this wouldn't be too much for her to take in a dream.

"Oh?" Gilly faltered a bit, afraid of what would come next. Nicolai's parents were great and had a love she could only envy but his father was a brute when it came to business and wanting Nicolai to follow his path.

She also thought he was being risking telling her this in a dream and not in person. What if she caught on to this being more than a dream? Well she already knew this was a shared dream and what was being said was real but he didn't know she knew.

"Yes and before you freak out, as I can already see I have startled you, it went well. He supports it. Supports us. They both do. Ma and Pops want me happy above all else. They said they just needed to see I could make the decision alone. Well I hope it's not completely alone...because well baby, I want you by my side always. My parents have given their blessing. They think you are the perfect match for me. They love you. I love you Sweetling."

Nicolai starred at her for what felt like forever. She just looked up at him, her blonde hair blowing in the breeze, her lips a deep red from her worrying them and her grayish blue eyes hauntingly silent.

"Gillyanna?"

Gilly couldn't believe what he had told her. His parents were okay with it? They were okay with her? She was so caught up in all of that it took a moment for her to realize what else he had said.

He wanted her by his side? Not behind him, not just an on looker but an equal to him! And he said he loved her...again...man! This was not what she was expecting at all. She was letting him control all of this. It was time she took the lead again. When he said her name like it was a question she finally checked back into the situation at hand.

"Li, that's wonderful! Of course I'll be by your side! I love you!" She threw herself into his arms and kissed him as deeply as he had before only she didn't let up. She needed her answers now before the dream was up. When he let out a growl and pulled her tight against him she shifted out of the clothes she had been wearing into a silk baby doll in his favorite color, red. She let her hands roam all over him, one in his hair, one started to run down his back only to have the shirt he wore in the way, she willed it go and he stood before her naked. She ground against him and when he grasped her firm and pressed her against his hardness. She changed their dream while he was lost in her touch. They were no longer in the clearing but back in his room on his bed. She loved her house over his any day but had to admit his bed was a lot better than hers.

With her on top of him she had him trapped, the only thing he could do to stop her was wake up.

She sat up and looked down at him; with that single move she made the little piece of lingerie she wore disappear. Sitting astride him naked she kissed him one last time and spoke.

"Nicolai, before this goes any farther I need to tell you something as well." She took a deep breath and held it while he looked over her face for any sign of what was to come.

"I am the incarnate of the Goddess Maeve, Goddess of War, Sexuality, and Intoxication. I am her mortal form on earth. With that being said, I know this is a shared dream. I know this is not our first one, I also know that the only way this is possible is if you are divine in some way or another and seeing as how the only God who pertains to this realm is the companion of my goddess that tells me you are the incarnate of the God Neit, God of Battle. Am I right?"

She let out a deep breath after the rush of words left her mouth. She starred down at his shocked face waiting for something, anything to happen.

The dream to dissolve and she wake alone, him to try to argue, anything. When he started to laugh a deep, rich laugh she hadn't heard in years she felt a little taken back.

"Sweetling, you are too clever for your own good sometimes. Of course that Goddess of yours must have caught on too. I knew Neit could never keep it from you both. Yes Gilly, I am Neit's incarnate just as you are Maeve's. You and I are destined to be together and even if we weren't it would be you I found in the end. You are the only one who can hold my heart."

With that he pulled her back down and kissed her. When she laughed light heartedly and returned his kiss tenfold he knew all was finally right for them. With that he let her make love to him like never before, driving both of them to new heights and wonders.

When he finally woke up he was alone in his bed, the sheets were thrown about and the scent of Gillyanna still lingered on his skin. He smiled to himself and decided it was time to let the dreams rest and find his woman. He would have her in person today. He knew all would be right for them now, if only he could say the same for Neit and Maeve. There was more to this story then they first thought. The Dagda was involved. Nicolai made a note to summon the Great Father and seek the help he would need.

There would be a battle on the horizon between the Goddess and her companion God, a battle for love.

Chapter 18

Maeve starred at Neit in disbelief. They had just spent another night in one another's arms making love like never before and now…now he was just being unreasonable! The truth had finally come out about Nicolai and Neit.

He told her he had always known about the boy, that the Dagda had foretold it when Nicolai's mother was still carrying the bairn. How was that possible? The Dagda hadn't even told her of

Gilly until after she was born and felt the connection herself.

What else had the Dagda played a hand in? He had apparently known about Nicolai and Gilly from the start. Meaning…Neit had known as well!

"How could you have kept that from me?"

Maeve could feel her anger cascading with every word. It was flowing out of her. The realm was starting to absorb it. The Goddess of war was out and she wasn't going to play nicely.

Neit had his back to Maeve and started to walk away, but then he remembered that he was the God of Battle. He had never stood against Maeve in her full War Goddess exposure but he felt he would have to here for the first time.

Maeve had coaxed the truth out of him through sex! She used her body to get what she wanted. He felt betrayed. He could see the anger welling up inside her and felt his own blood start to boil. He knew that when he turned back to face Maeve his eyes would be sporting their bursting gold hue. He could feel it as the beast of war inside him started to come alive.

It had been a long time since Maeve and he had been to this level of anger. The last time was in the heat of battle against an enemy, not each other. He whipped around to face Maeve and saw a flash of fear in her eyes; it was fleeting but had been there. It was enough to still the beast, if only slightly. He didn't want to scare her but he was so angry he couldn't help it.

"Me? You're angry with me for keeping something the Dagda had confided in me a secret until now? What about you? How dare you use sex against me! How dare YOU come here and treat what we shared as a weapon! I would have told you the truth, you only need ask. I was planning on telling you tonight but you didn't let me speak before you jumped my loins!"

His outburst had shaken the walls of the realm. He could feel the heat on his flesh and see the look of horror back in Maeve's eyes. He took control back over the monster of rage bubbling at the surface of his skin.

"I am sorry, I didn't mean to frighten you but your explosion of anger set me off. How can you be mad at me for keeping this to myself until the time was right? You know timing is everything with these things. How could you betray me like this? How could you use our love making against me? Does it mean that little to you?"

Maeve starred at Neit and felt her heart break. He was right. She had freaked out and acted without thinking. She never gave him a chance to explain why he had kept it to himself.

She also didn't go about the sex thing the way she should have. She should have been more subtle and she should have given him the chance to talk to her first but she wanted him so badly and couldn't control her lust. Now she looked at the man before her whose eyes were glowing gold, whose body was taut from tension and anger and felt as though she had just killed the most beautiful thing she had ever had. He sounded so defeated.

"Neit…I…you…I'm sorry." She couldn't find the words to say.

"You're sorry? That's all you have for me?" Neit was getting angry again. She thought she could say sorry and it would fix it?

"NO! Neit it wasn't supposed to be like this. I was just feeling so betrayed because you knew something so important to me and kept it to yourself. I wasn't trying to use our love making against you. I had every intention of letting you talk, of going about it right but when I got here all I could think about was feeling you against me." Maeve looked away.

She couldn't face him. She was so angry with herself now and the fact that he thought she would use him and their love making. She couldn't stand there and hear the judgment in his voice any longer either.

She needed to disappear. She messed up and was certain she lost him. She wasn't going to stick around just to find out she did.

"I love you Neit." With that she vanished from the realm and went to the only place she knew she could hide. Her castle in the realm of the Fey, her fairy people would hide her till she healed and nowhere else in the universe had the effect on her that her fairy realm had.

Even though she was a Goddess she also held the title of Queen of the Fey and while her presence

among her subjects wasn't required she did visit
the realm on occasion to check in with her
council there. Today she would surprise them
with an extended stay until her heart stopped
hurting. It was also the one place Neit

wouldn't be able to sense her, it also meant no
contact with Gilly for a while which she hated
but she couldn't think of another option

Neit looked up when her words reached his ears
only to see her fade away.

"Damn it!" Neit ran his fingers through his hair.
She finally said it loud enough for him to hear it

and with the intention of him hearing it but he didn't even get to return his love before she ran out on him.

"How can she even do that to me? She didn't even give me a chance to respond. To fix what was going on. She ran out on me!" Now he felt not only anger but a sadness he didn't think he could shake. He couldn't figure out why she would just walk away from here, no she didn't walk away she faded, she disappeared.

He couldn't even sense her anymore. She had

vanished and he couldn't figure out where she had gone. Things just got so much harder. How did he win her over when she would be avoiding him? How did he trust her again? This time he needed more than just Nicolai's help. He was going to have to go to Gilly. He would need her to get in touch with the Goddess and talk some sense into her. He finally had Maeve in his grasp and he let his anger chase her away.

"Please let me get her back." He didn't know if anyone could hear his plea but for now he would just have to seek out Gilly and Nicolai and hope that the Goddesses little angel could help him

out.

Chapter 19

Nicolai had just arrived at Gilly's house. He had gone over unannounced hoping to catch her off guard. There was only one car in the driveway which meant that Izett had returned to her uptown apartment for the night.

The only light on in the house was the one to Gilly's office in the rear of the house which could only mean one thing at this hour, she was writing. She was probably bunkered down in what anyone else would consider the most uncomfortable position writing up a storm and lost in her own little world. The house could be on fire and she wouldn't even notice. There could be a marching band playing next to her and she wouldn't hear a sound.

She had her quirks like that. She had this office, well it was more like a study or library really but it was a small room in the observatory of the house at the very back. It had one large window on the outmost wall that looked out into the woods with a clear view of the sky. The other three walls were covered in bookshelves that almost reached the ceiling. She had a spiral stair case that cascaded to the top of the shelves and a rolling ladder that would go from one side of the room to the other so she could skid her way to whatever book her heart desired most.

She would lock herself away in there, sitting on the bench in her little window haven and write for hours. When she would run out of things to write or hit a block she would simply stare out her window and wait for nature to inspire her. He loved that about her. A little whimsical maybe but something about it seemed magical even to him.

He got out of the car and made his way to the house. He would go in the front door just in case Maeve was there. If he was going to run into her he didn't want it to disturb Gillyanna. He was actually hoping she would be into her writing enough for him to just stand there in the silence with only the sound of her fingers hitting the keys interrupting the peace.

He used to do that all the time, something about watching Gilly work made him happy. Not in the "I am a man make me a sandwich" or "I am a total creep" kind of way but in the "something feels complete here" kind of way.

He would stand there and see how long it took her to realize he was watching. It didn't matter if she was writing or cooking. It never took her too long to feel his presence but tonight he was hoping it would take her long enough for him to build up the courage to go through with his plan.

He idly rubbed his fingers across the ring he had in his jacket pocket. It was floating around in there and he wanted to make sure he didn't lose it. He walked to the front door and used his key to let himself in; this time he remembered it so he wouldn't have to leave a note or call. As he walked into the house he could tell Maeve was nowhere to be seen. He had gotten use to the feel of a godly presence and hers was absent.

As he wandered down the hall towards Gilly's study he kept worrying the ring in his pocket trying not to freak himself out, he had proposed to her once before right? And she had accepted so he shouldn't be worried now. Especially since now it was all in the open. No more secrets.

The thing was this was real. The first one had been business but this engagement would be for the right reasons and be the foundation they started over on. He was also a little worried about his choice of rings. This wasn't the original two carat diamond ring he had placed on her hand before.

BATTLING FOR LOVE

This ring Neit helped him pick out. It was a Claddagh ring. Neit had explained it to him a few nights ago. Claddagh rings are tokens of love, loyalty and friendship from the old days in Ireland. They held a lot of meaning.

This one was gold with a single emerald in the shape of a heart to represent love; two gold hands cradled it to represent friendship and on top of it rested the crown of loyalty. It was a triple banded ring that had love, loyalty and friendship each engraved on a band. He wanted

Gilly to know that he loved her always, would be loyal to her and only her for the rest of their lives and that he considered her his best friend. He wanted to do this right. He just hoped that this ring would be acceptable for her.

He came to the study and slowly opened the door and just as he expected his Sweetling was nestled up in her little sanctuary typing away. He wondered what book she was working on, if she was influenced by anything or anyone special at the moment but he dared not step closer. He listened to the sound of her typing, her fingers skimming the keyboard and the clicking sound that seemed to have a pulse of its own.

He wasn't sure how long he had stood there watching her but all of a sudden it was quiet. She had stopped. She hadn't noticed him yet, instead she was staring up at the moon with a grin on her face. The light on the desk didn't light the room fully and didn't reach into her corner. She was lit by a mix of the moon and the glow of the computer before her. Her hair was shining in the light and her eyes bright and filled with a look of happiness. When she started to whisper to the moon he could feel himself being drawn to her like a moth to a flame.

"Thank you. Thank you for hearing my call to my goddess. Thank you for lighting my way in the darkness. Thank you for your strength and inspiration. Thank you for the handsome man standing in my door way right this moment."

BUSTED!

Nicolai simply stammered his pardon she laughed harder. "Did you really think I wouldn't feel you standing so near?"

"Near? Me? Why, I am all the way over here loving." Nicolai grinned widely and closed the distance between them and sealed their mixed laughter with a kiss.

Chapter 20

Gilly and Nicolai sat and talked for most of the night about all the things that had been going on over the last few months. His career, her book in the making and just life in general and how it had changed since the God and Goddess had come into their lives.

It was Nicolai's stomach rumbling that interrupted the conversation. They laughed about it and Gilly immediately jumped at the opportunity to cook for Nicolai. He had always loved her cooking which made her feel good about it.

They left the study to go into the kitchen still laughing together. Nicolai was walking behind her with his arms wrapped around her middle trying to step with her so that they moved as one.

It made walking a little more difficult and they stumbled a few times just bringing more laughter about. She loved how goofy he was. He had always found a way to make her laugh. When they got to the kitchen they parted their ways, Nicolai went to sit at the island counter and Gilly made her way to the refrigerator. Gilly started to raid her fridge to make something for them to eat and was quickly lost in her thoughts. Nicolai was still talking to her.

Telling her stories and old memories, he kept coming back to stories about them. The moments they were happiest, when he wasn't shut down on her.

BATTLING FOR LOVE

She was standing at the counter and her gaze moved to the window in front of her. She looked out at the woods and just took in all she saw; she liked to do that a lot. She was fascinated by the world around her and the things she didn't know and for some reason nature itself held a special place in her heart and mind. The way things grow and the beauty of everything around her captivated her.

She always found a way to see outside, especially when she had a lot on her mind that's why her house had a lot of windows in it so she could feed her habit.

It was relaxing. That's why she had bought this house off the beaten path. She was lost in herself as usual when she was suddenly wrapped in two strong arms. Nicolai had come up behind her and entwined her in his firm grasp. She let out a little sigh and leaned back into him when he kissed the hollow of her neck.

She liked this, having him so close. They stood like that for a while in silence, just looking out the window and enjoying each other. She felt like she had her best friend back, her other half, she was finally complete.

She was basking in their companionable silence when he kissed just behind her ear and then her cheek and finally his lips sought out hers. She moaned into his mouth and she pressed against him. Their lips moved together and their tongues did an expert dance, teasing and tasting every inch of one another's mouths. She drew his lip into her mouth and sucked on it dragging a breathless laugh from him. This is what she had been waiting for.

She was anxious the whole night waiting for a move, wondering if she should make it first. Their dreams had been wonderful torments, feeling real but nowhere near as tangible as this. This was heaven, perfection, raw passion. They were both panting when Nicolai broke the kiss. He leaned his head against hers and left a soft kiss on her forehead.

BATTLING FOR LOVE

She smiled up at him mesmerized by what she saw. It was a mix of pure unquestionable love, the kind you can see and feel with no words, and desire, untried and pent up.

It had her trapped. He just sat there smiling at her. He was quiet; it was a change from the past few hours of constant conversation. He looked like he was lost in his own thoughts. She wasn't sure what was going through his head at the moment but she knew no matter what ideas or plans were in the making she was on board. She wanted this man for life no matter what it took.

She couldn't shake the feeling of unease though. Something wasn't quite right.

He wasn't acting the same as he had only moments ago. It was like a shadow had moved over him within seconds. Was she wrong? Was he shutting down again? She couldn't take it if he did. It would kill her. Her heart would never heal.

"Sweetling," Nicolai looked down at her and could see a little sadness, it was like the clouds had moved in and blocked the sun. He felt a twinge on guilt for all he had done to her in the past but he pushed it aside. She had forgiven him. She said she understood and would never give up on him.

They could finally be happy together. "I love you."

"I love you Li, so very much." Nicolai had a waver in his voice she wasn't use to. It was a vulnerable sound..."What's wrong? You've gone all quiet on me."

Nicolai decided there was no point in putting it off anymore, there really wasn't a point putting it off in the first place. He had no reason to fear rejection. He could see how she felt in her eyes, feel it in her touch and was soothed by it in her voice. Now was the time.

He got down on one knee, pulled out the ring and looked up at Gillyanna.

"Gillyanna McFly. I want to do this right this time around. I love you, with all my heart and soul loving. I want you to know that I will spend the rest of our lives proving that to you. I will make up every wrong I have done and I vow to you that I will never hurt you again. You are everything, my one and only, my destiny. I was made to love you. There is no one in this world that will ever compare to you or hold my heart the way you do. You are the one thing in my life

I can't live without. You make me stronger and give me a reason to laugh and believe. I know this ring isn't as big as the last, but it holds so much more meaning for me. It is a Claddagh ring, an old traditional ring from Ireland. It symbolizes friendship, love and loyalty. To me there isn't a more perfect ring because I will love you, be loyal to you and be your best friend for the rest of our existence. Will you do me the greatest honor and make me the happiest man alive by becoming my wife?"

Nicolai stared into Gilly's eyes. He watched the tears start down her cheeks, the smile spread across her face and waited for what seemed like hours for her to answer.

Gilly was at a loss for words. Well actually she knew exactly what she wanted to say. She wanted to scream yes and jump up and down in a little happy dance. He was proposing and not like before, this was real. The tenderness is his eyes, the openness was astounding. He had her completely no questions asked. He didn't even need to ask her to be his wife; to herself she admitted she already was even if no vows were spoken. There could be no other man in the world to ever exist that would be able to call her his. Nicolai was the ultimate; the only, her hopes and dreams come to life. He was her equal in every way.

His first proposal had been adequate she guessed and the ring was gorgeous but didn't fit her style or personality like the one he held now did. He hadn't gotten down on one knee. He hadn't said half of the heartfelt things he had just said. He had merely sat her down, offered her his deal and asked her to be his partner. The ring was a two carat princess cut diamond set in a stunning platinum band but it was not the ring she had pictured she would wear on her ring finger.

She had always been more for colored gem stones like garnet and emerald over diamonds.

She liked classic yellow gold for a band or even a white gold. Of course he had known that long ago because she always stopped to look at jewelry when they would pass by a store, she loved jewelry and rings were her weakness. The Claddagh ring not only fit their heritage but was a perfect fit for her.

It was yellow gold with three bands. Each one had a row of small round diamonds but the heart of the ring was a stunning emerald, rich in color and depth. It was exactly what she would have picked for herself. He had made her dreams come true just now. She had her answer ready.

"Li? Does this mean you aren't hungry anymore?" She said with a smile that lit the whole room.

Nicolai jumped up and swept her into his arms and a kiss. She hadn't actually said the word yes but he knew she had meant it. It was her little goofball streak. She always made jokes.

This woman was his dreams come to life, his happiness, his everything, his bride to be. He felt complete for the first time in his life. He realized what Gilly was then, she was his Goddess.

"Oh I am hungry loving, but it's a different hunger." His gaze bore into Gilly sending heat coursing through her veins. She let out a husky laugh.

He swung her up in his arms, kissed her deeply and carried her away to the bedroom. He had enough of shared dreams. He didn't mind the dreams but now he had her in reach and it was time for him to love her in real life. He couldn't carry her up the stairs fast enough. Tonight he would love her into a stupor. Tomorrow he would take the steps with the love of his life and set about making her his wife. He would make her his one and only forever.

Chapter 21

Neit arrived at Gilly's house early that morning. He knew he shouldn't have but he popped into her bedroom where she and Nicolai were laying wrapped in one another's arms.

Gilly's head was resting on Nicolai's chest and the man wore the most content look upon his face as he ran his fingers through her hair. His eyes where closed but as soon as he sensed Neit's presence they opened.

Nicolai looked down at Gilly and back at Neit and anger first came to his eyes only to be stifled. He covered Gilly up more and woke her gently. She made a sound of disgust and swatted his arm. Neit laughed at her action which only resulted in her panic.

"What?" Gilly jumped instantly. She was lying against Nicolai and hadn't felt his chest vibrate with laughter which told her someone else was in the room. She looked up at Nicolai to see him staring past her and nodding. She turned her head to see a gorgeous man standing in the bedroom and at first she was too dazed to look away or think. No man should be that handsome. Then she realized she wasn't looking at a man. She was looking at a God.

She could feel his presence and something in her shuddered when she realized she hadn't heard from her Goddess. Something wasn't right. She knew the God before her was it was Neit,

Maeve's companion, yet where was Maeve? "Hello, Neit. May I ask why you are in my bedroom?"

"Neit do you think you could step out and give us a chance to get dressed. Then we will discuss what brings you here."

"Um, sure. However one favor. Gillyanna? When did you last feel Maeve's presence?"

"Don't you mean when don't I feel her presence? She's here now" Gilly laughed a little at the God. What did he mean by that? She was the incarnate of the Goddess Maeve for crying out loud. She always felt her Goddess...wait, no something was wrong. She couldn't feel Maeve.

She called out to her and got no response. Not a single word. She started to panic. Neit was starting to walk away and he had a look in his eye. He looked sad, and guilty.

"Neit hang on a second…I don't feel her here. What's going on? Where is she? What have you done you oaf?" Gilly was getting angrier by the syllable.

She realized she hadn't felt Maeve's presence and connection since last night sometime. Maeve was supposed to be with Neit…something was terribly wrong.

"Right well, that is why I am here. I will give you two a moment but please hurry. The longer she is away the harder this will be. I think I lost her." Neit's voice was full of remorse. He was completely defeated.

Gilly watched him walk away looking less like a God and more like a man with no hope. It broke her heart and scared her. What had happened to him and Maeve? What scared her the most was that she couldn't feel Maeve anymore.

This couldn't be good. Why would her Goddess disappear on her? She jumped out of bed and immediately got dressed. She didn't wait for Nicolai to join her. Instead she ran down the stairs to talk to Neit.

"What has happened Neit? All of it I need to know all that was said. We need to find her."

Neit sat down and told what had happened; the argument, his mistakes, Maeve's mistakes and parting words. After he finished tell Gillyanna all that had happened he felt even more depressed than before.

He had always thought the worst feeling in the world to be loving Maeve and not

being able to tell her until now. Living with that secret had been torture to him for many millennia, but this, this was even more painful than anything he had ever felt.

He finally told her that he loved her. Finally he had opened up to her just to feel betrayed and then lost her. There wasn't anything in the universe, not another thing in existence that would hurt as much as the pain he felt in his chest now.

He hadn't been able to look at Gilly during his confession but now he met her strong gaze and saw that she looked just as sad as he felt.

"Please do not pity me Gilly."

"Neit I do not pity you. This being our first meeting and conversation I do not wish to sound rude but I don't feel sorry for you at all. I am sad because I understand exactly how you feel. I can see the sadness inside you and I wish it gone. It is not pity. It is sympathy for a man who deserves to love and who loves a woman who loves him back, a woman who just so happens to be the goddess that I am connected to. She didn't just disappear on you Neit, she left me too."

"I know she did. I don't want you to think I am on some selfish mission. I cannot imagine how you feel now that she has left but I need your help getting her back, for both of our sake. I will be indebted to you for a life time. Anything you wish is yours."

Neit was graveling he knew but he needed her help. She would have to be the one to get Maeve back. He still planned on going to the Dagda for back up but even he wouldn't be able to make Maeve return. It would have to be Gilly.

"Neit stop begging please. I need her too. I am in this with you." Gilly looked at the god before her and realized that he was her. He loved Maeve and had never been able to really express it much like she had been with Nicolai. She couldn't walk away from the God.

Neit was so excited to hear Gilly's words he leapt up, swept her into his arms and started to spin her around in circles. Her laughter filled his ears and for the first time all day he felt hope.

Her laughter was contagious and he felt his own start to bubble up from deep within. When it erupted from within he almost didn't recognize the sound. How long had it been since he had laughed so truly?

"I must thank you. You seem to be the key to happiness around here. I can see why Nicolai is always smiling and laughing. I can see why Maeve finally feels at home. Thank you for accepting and welcoming me into your life as well." Neit looked at her and smiled.

This woman was spectacular. Her happiness and hope was contagious to all around her. Nicolai was a lucky man no question asked.

"Well thank you Neit, I consider myself lucky too. Now will you please set my fiancée down so that I may kiss her good morning and then we can set to work on what needs to be done to find our missing goddess? Gilly call Izett you two are going to both be needed for this and Neit I have a feeling that you may need to make a trip to see the big man upstairs and I mean literally. The Dagda is waiting for you in the guest bedroom. Good luck."

Chapter 22

Neit tried not to lose his composure at Nicolai's words. The Dagda was here? That couldn't be good. Why would the God show up here?

Unless…oh this could only mean that something was terribly wrong and considering the recent events with Maeve it wasn't a real surprise.

Perhaps the Dagda will have some answers. Now is not the time to panic.

"The Dagda? THE DAGDA? In my house? Oh can I meet him please? PLEASE?" Gilly was bouncing up and down like a little kid. She was grinning ear to ear. The excitement radiating off her was almost tangible.

"Gilly I don't think that is such a great idea. If he is here it is not for the joy of a visit." Nicolai looked at her sternly but his gaze was boring into the back of her head because she was already off running up the stairs. His eyes drifted to her backside as it wiggled its way away from him.

He caught himself at the sound of Neit chuckling, "You think it wise that she go up there unescorted?"

"Why not? She is under the protection of a Goddess who is a daughter under the Dagda. After all you apparently have had your solitude with him. Am I correct?"

"Well yes of course I did otherwise I wouldn't have been the one to tell you that he was here."

"And did he speak of anything private to you? Anything you must keep to yourself?"

"Well, yes he did. What does that have to do with the women I love running up to see him all alone?"

"Maybe he has words to share with her. Did you every think that?"

"Oh um, no I didn't. You are right Neit. I'll give her a moment. Then you can have your words with the Dagda while Izett and Gilly speak. Izett should be on her way over now."

Gilly reached the door to the room that the Dagda was behind and she paused for the first time in her accent. After all the Dagda was here, he is the Father of them all. She was giddy and silly with excitement. She thrust open the door and bound into the room.

She stop abruptly, he was there. Standing in front of her looking right at her wearing a crooked smile that was both breathtakingly beautiful and unnerving was the Dagda. He was an older man; his wisdom could be seen in his eyes. He looked that of an older man but there was a hint of the young rouge he had been at one time.

There was no doubting that this had been the God to turn heads, mostly the heads of woman who were captivated by the large taut muscles of his chest and arms. His once dark auburn hair was now highlighted by streaks of silver and white, his beard matching that of the hair on his head. His eyes were a haunting deep blue. She could feel the power coming off him. What got her most was his voice. When he spoke it was like everything else around her disappeared.

His voice was deep, powerful and admittedly a little husky, like it was laden with pleasure and desire. For some reason though she doubted that it was because of her presence. Something told her that was simply his voice.

"Why hello Gillyanna, it is nice to finally meet you." He spoke simply and as if he was greeting a friend. It shocked Gilly a little. After all she had just barged uninvited into the room that he had commandeered in her house and he was the Good God, the all Father.

"H-h-hello Dagda." Gilly lost her voice and strength when it came her turn to talk.

"Sit down if you will. We have some things to discuss if you will and please do not be intimidated. I have looked forward to the day we might meet. It is not every day that a mortal has the strength and power to best two of my gods, especially when one of those gods is the Goddess

Maeve. She is not known for being easily bested."

Gilly nodded and went to sit on the window seat in the guest room. She had one of these in every room in case she needed to hide away. Not that she needed to very often in her own home but sometimes the view outside the window opened her eyes and imagination to so much more and the same view from her study day after day no matter how beautiful sometimes lead to a need for a change of scenery.

"I am glad to see that you are not completely lost on your own. I knew you would find your way and I cannot tell you how happy it makes me to know you and Nicolai have finally come together and I can promise you that no more struggles will come your way when it comes to you both."

"Thank you so much." Gilly's face lit up with pure delight. She had a feeling it would that way but having the Dagda tell her and confirm it only made it all the more real.

"You are quite welcome. Now to more serious matters, Maeve is not really missing so much as she is hiding in another realm. One where she can hide behind jovial music and dancing. Her fairies make for a great distraction. It is impossible to track her there because there is no way of sensing an immortals presence, which also means that if you and Izett are able to find it Neit can help get you there."

"Well that is good news but how do we find where the realm exists?"

"That is something that only the daughter and incarnate of a goddess can know."

"So you mean that Izett and I have the answer but we do not know it yet? Will we find it?"

"Yes, you will. Now I cannot tell you more but I am glad that we were able to talk. I hope I have helped you enough. And speaking of Izett...I know you worry about her but I promise you that there is a greater plan for her then what you see now."

"More than you know. I think we can figure it out relatively quick. Thank you Dagda."

"You are welcome daughter. Now go I must speak with Neit and I have a feeling the God is in my internal peril than any of us believe."

"If it is alright to say, I know what he is feeling. I do understand what he is feeling. I also know how to help him, if you will let me."

"Yes I will. Good luck daughter. Now I can hear the men ascending the stair case which means I have kept you too long; one is impatient and wants you back in his arms, the other is impatient and wants to know why I am here."

"Okay, okay I will go now. Izett should be here any moment as is." Laughing Gilly turned to the door and opened it just as Neit raised his fist to knock.

"Good timing!" Gilly gave Neit a dazzling smile. As she walked past him she gave his arm a reassuring squeeze. She kept walking though right into Nicolai's arms. Neit couldn't hold back a smile of his own. They truly were perfect together. They balanced one another and brought out each other's best qualities. They also challenged one another when it was called for.

He could only hope to be so lucky but of course that made him think of Maeve and how he had lost her, which then lead to him thinking about the fact that the Dagda was waiting inside the room for him. He turned to face the Good God hoping that he wouldn't be walking away from this feeling more lost then he was. He needed answers. He also needed to keep the anger he was feeling under control. After all part of

Maeve's overreaction was because the Dagda had never told her about Nicolai and Gillyanna's destiny and yet Neit had known from the day Nicolai came to be. It did seem to be unjust. Why had the Dagda kept that from Maeve?

"Neit, we have much to discuss please close the door behind you. Gilly, Nicolai I will being seeing you my children. Take care. Good luck in your search." With those last words Neit was lost behind the bedroom door. The last Nicolai could see was a weak attempt at a reassuring smile on Neit's face.

Chapter 23

Maeve sat on looking at her Faerie subjects running around laughing, dancing and truly enjoying themselves. She tried to smile but like it has been with every celebration among her court here in her realm of Fey, where there was cause for celebration just for waking each morning, she wasn't able to immerse herself into the fun because her hearts constant pain kept her mind elsewhere. How was it possible for this pain to still exist? She should have been able to move on; she looked at her sentry and men at arms.

They all glanced back at her as if they could feel her eyes on them.

They all wore the same look, that of desire and want. She knew they would be willing to please her, they would fight for the chance and while she had been known to take a few as lovers in the past she just wasn't interested. They were all handsome and all had the build of warriors but the only warrior she desired and wanted was Neit.

As soon as she thought of him her heart tightened in her chest. It was strange to her. It hurt more than anything she had ever felt before yet it still made her heart leap just thinking of his smile.

She missed everything about him. She missed the sound of his voice, the feel of his arms, his lips on hers, the way their bodies fit together and the way he made her feel. Her pain was accompanied by guilt too. Guilt about the words she parted with, guilt about hiding here because she knew he wouldn't be able to find her and her guilt went deeper.

She had run out on Gilly too. Gilly had overcome so much to have Maeve in her life and

Maeve didn't even have the decency to stay in that life. She left Izett too, Izett, who had just started to come out of her shell and prove herself as a woman of spirit. The great Goddess of War was hiding away licking her wounds.

She wished she could go back to that day and redo it. She had spent the past two months dwelling on that day and how she wanted to take back the words she had used.

She wanted to look Neit in the eyes and claim her love. She had thought many times about checking in on her incarnate and daughter but if she had done so she would have given away her location. The only being outside of her Fey to know the location of her glade was The Dagda. She trusted him not to reveal the whereabouts of her haven but she didn't trust him not to interfere in some way. Of course if he had told the others where she would hide they would have come by now right?

Maybe they weren't looking for her. She wouldn't blame them honestly. She had run out on everyone who had ever meant something to her and they probably hated her for it. She sat in her self-pity for a few moments longer before she was drawn out by a familiar voice. Only it was not a voice she had heard in what seemed like more time than she could remember. The funny thing was the voice made Maeve smile and drug her out of a deep sadness but she barely caught the voice, it was a mere whisper that was not even directed to her.

"Damn, Gilly do you see those warrior guys? No wonder Maeve has been hiding here. Think she will let me join her?"

"Shh, Izett knock it off, we have to find Maeve. Keep your pants on. Besides Maeve wouldn't take any lovers while she was here. She loves

Neit, we both know this."

"Yea I know, but can you blame me? They don't make men like this in St. Louis, at least in all the years we have lived in and around the place I have yet to see such perfection. Anyways, I haven't had the luck you and Maeve have had. This girl right here? She isn't getting any. My vibrator is probably about to commit suicide for over use."

"Oh goddess Izett that's hilarious and disturbing. Now be quiet you are a terrible ninja. I thought you said you could sneak like a shadow?"

"Yea well, I lied. I just really wanted to come on the 'rescue Maeve' mission."

"Fair enough, it is kind of cool. Now can we find Maeve and drag her ass home?"

Maeve listened and laughed in silence. Her girls were the best and they had found her. If she was correct they were in the trees behind her which would explain Izett's reaction to the sentry.

She was debating on letting them keep searching for her but she decided she had missed them too much and needed to see them now. It didn't mean however that she wasn't going to do so her way and play along. She wanted them to know she had known they were there.

"Can I kick and scream the whole way? Oh and if you are dragging can you avoid water, mud and any other unmentionable disgusting thing that would make a mess of me?" Maeve spoke as she walked around her dais to see that she was correct her ladies were right behind her.

Gilly and Izett stopped dead in their tracks, pivoted and let out the most joyful yet ear shattering screech in unison. They ran to Maeve and the woman embraced in tears and laughter. For the first time in months Maeve felt her heart heal. She was happier than she had been since the moment she had accused Neit. The only thing that could possibly make this reunion any better would be if Neit had been there.

Since the girls had been the one to make the trip to come and find her. Since they had been the ones to track her down and go through the trouble of finding her hidden glen she could only assume that meant that Neit had not forgiven her.

"Well my dearest love, that would be the worst assumption in the history of time. I forgave you before you ever left. I have been hunting for you from the moment you left with those last few parting words." He spoke as he slid his arms around her and pulled her close. "You should never have left, but now that I have you I will never let you go. I love you Maeve please come home with me."

Maeve could do little more than nod her head as she lost herself in his eyes. The rush of relief, love and true desire that flushed through her left her speechless. He had come. He loved her. He wanted her home with him. As those thoughts flooded her mind she threw herself into his arms and kissed him. Tears were streaking her face but she didn't care she had her love back and she wasn't going to make the mistake of walking away ever again.

Chapter 24

Nicolai was pacing in the living room, the sound of the TV inaudible and droning in the background. He had agreed to be the one to stay behind incase Maeve would come back for some reason.

They had started planning their rescue mission from the moment Izett had arrived after Maeve's disappearance. It had taken nearly two months to study all of the myths of Maeve and her fey, compare geographical maps and descriptions of wooded areas around them to see where they would be most comfortable, learn how to tell the fey from mortals, find a fey, track the fey back to the place where the grove existed, and then learn the way to cross into the hidden place.

All the while Nicolai had to be the one to sit back and not act just in case Maeve has come home. What he wasn't expecting was the hug he received from the Goddess when she saw him after everyone returned to the house. He wasn't sure of her feelings towards him after what he had put Gilly through but he had assumed she would be angry with him. It seemed he was wrong though, she accepted him and congratulated him and Gilly on their engagement and told him she was proud of the man he had become.

"Thank you Maeve. It really means a lot to me to hear you say that." And he meant it. Maeve had the most influence on Gilly and he wanted to know there was no animosity going into their new life. "Neit I think now would be the time to tell the women what we talked about, yes?"

"You are right my son. Why don't you tell Gilly here…and I will take Maeve to our realm and tell her there. See you all tomorrow." With a devilish grin Neit grabbed Maeve and they both disappeared from the room.

"Hey! Tell us what? Neit? Don't you keep her too long. You're not the only one who has missed her!" Gilly was yelling at the ceiling wearing one of her all too beautiful smiles.

When she turned back to her friend and her fiancée they both wore smiles. Nicolai was looking at her in a way that made her blush and she knew he would see it so she turned her attention to Izett.

She too wore a smirk but it didn't reach her eyes.

She was looking between Gilly and Nicolai with a hauntingly sad longing that Gillyanna could only assume was because Izett was feeling like the odd man out.

After all Gilly and Nicolai had fixed their differences and were back on track to getting married, this time because they both wanted it out of love. Neit and Maeve were off fixing their problems now and on their way to blissful happiness as well.

Then there was Izett, still the only one looking for what people spend their whole lives longing for. They really needed to see to it that Izett found happiness. After all she had done for Gilly and Maeve it was only right. Gilly thought about this for what seemed like the millionth time over the past couple months. Slowly Izett started to seem defeated by her solitude.

It wasn't that Izett needed a man to be happy but it didn't hurt to have someone to love, cherish, call your best friend, bicker with, make love to and know without a doubt there would be no end to the things they could share. Maeve and Gilly had talked about it quite a few times before the Goddess had left.

All Maeve could tell her was there was a plan for Izz, hell that's what the Dagda told her too. She couldn't help but wonder what that plan was though.

"Izz, are you okay?"

Izett had been zoned out like never before. She was happy to have Maeve back and see that she and Neit were doing better. She was happy Gillyanna and Nicolai were better than ever and that the wedding was right around the corner.

Everything around her was happy and wonderful but she was sad. She was envious too. The little green monster of jealousy kept poking its head about and she was fighting it. She didn't want her solemn attitude to affect those around her.

She really needed to talk to Gilly about something though. She hadn't told her about it yet because everything else seemed so much more important but she kept having a strange reoccurring dream. In her dream a man like one she had never seen before would approach her. His dark eyes would pierce her and he would hold her gaze for what felt like hours. They were black pits but there seemed to a glow in them, like the light was barely being held back.

It would startle her and she would think of running but couldn't and then as if he could read her thoughts he would give her a chilling smirk that made her heart race and blood run cold. He had hair that was black as night that fell past his shoulders. His skin was fair but fell taut and strong over his sharp features and muscles. He was a beautiful man. In her dream she would think of him as a vampire (she really needed to start reading other books before bed) but again as if reading her mind he would smile wider and laugh the most hearty, deep, rich laughter she had ever heard. It was like sunlight peeking through the dark clouds.

Everything about this man drew her in. The only words he ever spoke to her were the same time and time again. "My dear sweet Red, I am coming for you. You don't know how you torment me. I have never wanted someone so badly and yet I cannot have you? Why does your torturing of me have to be so sweet?"

Then he would kiss her in a way that she had never been before. The kind of kiss that made every other kiss in the history of the universe seem so bland. The worst part is that she would wake up as soon as his lips would leave hers and his parting words would echo through her.

"Just like a fire. Light, hot and melting me to the bone".

She would stare into the dark but she couldn't shake the feeling that he was still there, like a shadow hiding from the light. Damn dream man, making her want things she can't have. She really needed to tell Gillyanna about this though. She wasn't sure why but Gilly needed to know

"Izz?"

"Oh yea Gilly, we need to talk alone. Please? And grab some damn wine. We are going to need it."

Gilly looked at Nicolai, shrugged and gave him a kiss before following Izett into the study.

Izett slammed the door shut behind Gilly and started pacing. She didn't even give Gillyanna a chance to speak she just barked an order to poor he wine and after downing the first glass in a gulp she went on a rant about her dream man. When she was done she was breathless and panting. To her surprise Gilly just started to laugh so hard that her cheeks were streaked with tears.

Chapter 25

Nicolai and Neit stood together looking around the clearing. Everything was perfect and all of the guests were starting to arrive. They had been a little worried about how a double wedding was going to work when half of the guest list was made up of gods but it seemed to be working well.

The only thing out of the ordinary was how perfect the gods looked among mortals.

When Maeve had said yes to Neit's proposal they had all agreed that a double wedding would be the way to go. The planning had gone fairly smoothly. Izett had been made maid of honor to both of the women and Neit had called on his closest friend Llew to be man of honor.

Nicolai's mother and father were sitting in the first row and despite the chance of exposure the Dagda had agreed to be the man to give away both Maeve and Gilly. Everything was ready. They had chosen the clearing because this small secluded space behind Gillyanna's house had meaning for all four of them. It was were Gilly and Nicolai first made love, where Gilly had called upon Maeve, where Neit had realized that Nicolai was finally ready for a life of divinity and so much more.

Yellow ribbons and roses decorated the field and an archway stood behind them when the minister waited to start the service. Everything was so bright and beautiful and Nicolai couldn't wait for the day to start. The only thing left was for the women to come walking up the aisle. The men stood waiting trying to be patient. Sweat beaded their foreheads as they waited.

Nicolai kept looking at Llew there was something eerie about the man in a haunting way yet he still looked like the nicest man you would ever meet so long as you don't piss him off.

Llew was acting oddly too. He kept staring at the spot where the women would be coming toward them and Nicolai couldn't figure out why. The man was a mystery and Nicolai just knew that Neit trusted him so he would do the same.

Nicolai's thoughts were lost to him when the small orchestra started to play their music. He turned his attention away from Llew and to the isle. Izett was making her way towards them. She looked beautiful in her yellow bridesmaid gown. Everything was perfect.

He was starting to get even more anxious because seeing Izett meant that his Gilly would soon be by his side. He heard a sharp intake of breath next to him and turned his head to see Llew staring at Izett like he had seen a ghost. Llew wasn't taking his eyes off Izett.

When Nicolai looked back at Izett she was oblivious to the man staring at her. Izett was looking at people in the crowd and smiling. When she finally turn her attention in front of her she looked at Nicolai and smiled, then doing the same to Neit she was met with a smile in return. Finally her gaze fell on Llew and Nicolai noticed that she faltered a bit.

When Llew smiled right at her Izett tripped over herself. She looked stunned. Nicolai smiled and realized that as always in the presence of gods there was something greater going on here.

Izett could have died just then. Everything around her was perfect. Maeve and Gillyanna looked stunning and Izett had to admit she looked pretty damn good in the gown Maeve had the fey design for her, creative little darlings that they are. Izett was looking around at all the faces as she walked forward. On one side she was greeted by familiar faces and smiles. On the other side she was met by more smiles but the faces were as unfamiliar as could be but they were beautiful.

The gods and goddess in the group were exquisite. She had never seen so many striking people. She looked to Nicolai and could see

his happiness radiating off him and she could see the anxiety too. Neit wore the same look and she couldn't help but smile. They looked like the happiest men in the world at the moment and she couldn't wait to see their reaction to Gilly and Maeve.

At last her gaze fell on the man standing to the side of Nicolai and Neit. Her heart almost leapt from her chest. It was him, the man from her dreams. He was real? Izett tripped over herself for a moment. She needed to compose herself.

Gilly was the only one who knew of him. Surely this was a trick of the mind. Her dream man couldn't be real but the way he was looking at her made her question everything. He looked at her with recognition. The knowing in his eyes haunted her but she decided that she wouldn't let it show.

Today was for Maeve and Gilly. She would keep her calm until later. She walked past the men and then all the attention was focused behind her. Gilly and Maeve were coming up the aisle each of them with an arm looped through an arm of the Dagda. Both looked beautiful in separate ways.

Maeve was wearing an off white gown that flowed around her curves and accented every shape. It hung loosely around her shoulders and her long red hair draped in its wild abandon. She was an angel glowing in simplicity as she glided forward; eyes locked unwaveringly so on Neit.

Whereas Gilly's gown was more elaborate. It was the same off white color with black lace trim that also hung off her shoulders but clung to her bodice and waist and then flowed out like a ball gown, she too had her gaze locked onto her future husband.

They looked mesmerizing. They entire crowd took in a breath at the same time and went silent. There was nothing more beautiful in the entire universe at that moment. Izett finally returned her gaze to the best man only find him staring at her and smiling. It was as if he hadn't even noticed that the brides had arrived. The way he looked at her made her want to drop everything and walk into his arms. After that thought crossed her mind he smiled wider and more brilliantly and her mind with flooded with images that should have made her blush.

Izett didn't really remember the rest of the ceremony. It all happened so fast. By time she was able to break her gaze from the handsome stranger Gilly, Nicolai, Neit and Maeve were all walking back up the aisle and the Dagda was inviting everyone back to the house for the reception. Izett blinked and pulled it together and proceeded back up the aisle standing next to her handsome stranger.

"You look stunning Red." His voice wrapped her in a cloak of warmth.

"E...e...excuse me?" Izett lost all the control she had managed to gain. He had called her Red...that was the name the man in her dreams had called her.

"Do not act surprised. You recognized me instantly. I knew you were close to Maeve and Neit but I had never expected finding you to be so easy. I told you I would come for you." As he spoke he moved closer to her. His arm around her waist, his lips against her ear and the pure scent of man invaded her senses.

"It is you. How? Why? What do you want from me?" Izett was starting to panic.

"I want the one thing I was robbed of so many years ago. I want the one woman that I desire, the one woman I have waited for to break my curse, the one woman to be my light, heat and strength. I want you Izett." With that he kissed her cheek and walked away leaving her to her thoughts.

Izett stopped where she was and put a hand to her cheek where she could still feel the warmth of his kiss.

"Well shit. I guess you should be careful what you ask for when it comes to the gods…damn the Celtic Law…"

CPSIA information can be obtained
at www.ICGtesting.com
Printed in the USA
FFOW05n1306070716